T0363233

Talking Up

Young Women's Take
On Feminism

Talking Up

Young Women's Take
On Feminism

edited by

Rosamund Else-Mitchell
& Naomi Flutter

SPINIFEX

Spinifex Press Pty Ltd
504 Queensberry Street
North Melbourne, Vic. 3051
Australia
women@spinifexpress.com.au
http://www.spinifexpress.com.au/~women

First published by Spinifex Press, 1998

Copyright © on the collection Rosamund Else-Mitchell
and Naomi Flutter, 1998
Copyright © on individual pieces remains with the individual authors

All rights reserved. Without limiting the rights under copyright reserved
above, no part of this publication may be reproduced, stored in or
introduced into a retrieval system, or transmitted, in any form or by
any means (electronic, mechanical, photocopying, recording or otherwise), without prior written permission of both the copyright own-
ers and the above publisher of the book.

Copying for educational purposes:
Where copies of part or the whole of the book are made under part
VB of the Copyright Act, the law requires that prescribed procedures
be followed. For information, contact the Copyright Agency Limited

Extract from *It Could Have Been You* © Merlyn Nuttall and Sharon
Morisson printed with permission of Virago Press.

Typeset in Meta and Stone Informal
Page design by Julie Hunt
Cover design by Deb Snibson, Modern Art Production Group
Made and printed in Australia by Australian Print Group

National Library of Australia
Cataloguing-in-Publication data:

Talking Up: young women's take on feminism.

ISBN 1875559663.

1. Feminism – Australia. 2. Feminists – Australia. I. Else-Mitchell,
Rosamund, 1970–. II. Flutter, Naomi, 1970–.
305.420994

This Project has been supported by the Australia Foundation for
Culture & the Humanities.

For Margaret Brewster

Florence Flutter & Willma Wallace

Acknowledgements

There are many without whose help we could not have published this book. Our sincere thanks to Spinifex Press who have seen us through this long project. Both Susan Hawthorne and Jo Turner saw the value in a different kind of book about young women and feminism when it was just an idea. They have helped focus and guide us. Without Jo's hours of energy, dedication and friendship, there would be no *Talking Up*. We are grateful for the opportunity to work with and learn from her. Thanks also to Nikki Anderson, Maralann Damiano and Libby Fullard at Spinifex; to the designer, Deb Snibson and typesetter, Julie Hunt whose patience is so appreciated. During final stages, Hans van Leeuwen and Jo Turner's attention to detail and wisdom were invaluable.

Both of us have worked many jobs in the course of *Talking Up*. At all times we have been fortunate to receive assistance and support in various forms from supervsiors and peers. Our thanks particularly to Martin Smith's Bookshop, the Children's Book Council (NSW), SCEGGS Darlinghurst and La Trobe University's School of Law and Legal Studies.

Our families, friends and mentors have played a critical role through constant, gentle prodding, support and advice; thank you to Margaret Brewster, John Flutter, Sue-Anne Wallace, Chloe Flutter, Beverley McGaw, Bev Laurie, Stuart Thomas, Andrew Hewish and David Cavenor.

The names of all the young women involved in this project since its inception do not appear on the table of contents, their's and other's interest and input at various stages has helped to shape this book. These include: Claire Barbato, Natasha Cica, Gillian Cosgrove, Penny Duckworth, Sophie Gee, Bridget Gilmour-Walsh, Zoe Hart, Michelle Hollywood, Heidi James, Kathy Laster, Sally McCausland, Kate Pearcy, Jayne Pilkington, Padma Raman, Anna Reynolds, Indira Rosenthal, Louise Sampson, Bernice Smith, Nadine Smith, Fiona Stagger, Zoe St John and Sarah Todd.

We also gratefully acknowledge financial assistance from the Australia Foundation for Culture & the Humanities.

Finally, it is our contributors we wish to acknowledge for their sustained honesty, patience and good humour. Throughout, reading and listening to their stories has convinced us of the value of this project.

Contents

Voices: Mapping the Self

Acting Up

. . . so many of the stories that I write,
that we all write, are my mother's stories.

Alice Walker

Introduction

This collection answers the challenge issued to young feminists in 1995 by Anne Summers in a now-famous question: "Where are the books or the articles by young Australian women setting out their thoughts, seizing control of the debates, tweaking the noses of the old guard?" Anne Summers dared young women to talk back. As one of the gatekeepers of public debate, she tossed us the key and beckoned. However, we do not wish to "seize control", nor "tweak noses", nor declare our feminisms newer, better or more relevant than those of older women. This book captures our thoughts about how and why we became feminists.

Talking Up does not claim to be representative of all young women, nor does it claim to be radical. It is not an academic text, although some of its contributors have studied and taught feminist theory and Women's Studies at university. It is not the new activists' guidebook. It is a book in which twenty-one young Australian women affirm that the personal is political; and that it is usually in our personal lives, and in spite of privilege, education or social change, where our feminist consciousness begins. In reflecting upon their experiences, these twentysomething young women see the significance of feminism everywhere. They live their feminism each day. Some are talkers, others strategists, many are engaged with actual movements. All however, are interventionist, whether in their travel, their study, their jobs or their writing. They engage here with varyingly politicised aspects of feminism to produce interpretations and understandings of feminism that are simultaneously social, personal and political. Integral to their lives as feminists are issues of representations of women, the use of language, the right of access and equity, the right to choose, to love, or to leave are continually on our minds and in our actions.

We started talking about this collection in 1995, only then it was just talking; this book is the outcome of "living feminism". It was March and *The First Stone*, a fictionalised retelling of actual events that took place in 1993, had just been published. The book centres around two young women at Ormond College, a residential college at the University of Melbourne, who accused the College Master of sexual harassment. The college did not deal with the complaint effectively, and in the complainants' efforts to seek acknowledgment and redress, the alleged incidents took on a life of their own. The "layeredness" of the whole episode is still haunting: the alleged events one night at a college "smoko", the legal proceedings and a media frenzy; Garner's

impassioned letter to the Master, and a bizarre weaving of
her life with that of the protagonists. Finally, publication of
their story, without them, punctuated by Garner's own
reflections – and wall-to-wall exposure.[1]

Suffice to say that lots of women were talking about "that
case", "those women", "that feminist", in cafes, on buses, at
work and, of course, in universities. Back in 1995, we contacted some women we knew through study, through student
politics and other networks in Sydney, Melbourne and
Canberra. We wanted to respond publicly, first to Helen
Garner, then to Anne Summers. We wanted them to know
that feminism was alive and kicking. How best? After some
informal get-togethers in Canberra and Sydney, we struck
upon an ambitious plan: twenty young, new writers, few of
whom knew each other, busy studying, beginning careers,
would respond to *The First Stone* using it as a springboard to
a discussion about their relationships with feminism. We
discovered it was a risky idea. Who were we? What was the
"angle"? "Too academic", one publisher told us. "We already
have a young, feminist title", another said. "Who are the
names?" asked everyone. We have since taken great pleasure
in answering: "no-one you've ever heard of". While some of
our contributors might think this a little unfair, this response
addressed the assumption that books like this should include
some "usual suspects", as though declarations of feminism
require an established public profile.

In the course of this project, over forty young women
have been directly involved, and many others have been

---

1   Unfortunately, we do not have the space, or really the inclination, to line
    up the parties, to survey the accusations and counterarguments.
    Generation f, by Virginia Trioli (1996) and *bodyjamming*, Jenna Mead's
    1997 anthology about feminism and public life, both provide excellent
    overviews of *The First Stone* debates, issues and personalities.

interested and supportive. We would love to have printed all their stories. Some of these papers were recommended by initial contributors, some were delivered at a variety of conferences, forums, poetry nights, others were written to put across a single burning concern. However, not everyone had time; others decided that their support was best shown tacitly; others didn't want to put their feminist values on paper; and not everyone met the deadlines – as endlessly fluid as they were!

This book does not seek to cover all the complexities of feminist identity politics – which some may see as distinctly "unfeminist". But we were keen to resist any tokenism. This was to be a book of constructive conversations about feminism, using personal experiences and reflections as explanatory canvasses. We recognise that our individual voices will not "change the world", but we hope that they take their place within broader feminist debates in Australia.

In *Generation f: Sex, Power & the Young Feminist*, Virginia Trioli eloquently captures the impact of feminism on many dimensions of young women's lives today. She examines the significance of the 1994 AGB McNair telephone poll in which seventy per cent of young women polled in Sydney and Melbourne said they would not call themselves feminists. Trioli highlighted the paradox implicit in these numbers. Of course they believe in equal pay, a fair justice system, harassment-free workplaces and sexual freedom. This then raises several questions. What do the seventy per cent call these beliefs, if not feminism? And amongst the thirty per cent who "identify" as feminists, what else (if anything) do they see as feminist? (1996, p. 48) It seems as though the term is up for grabs. If we and many of our contemporaries were simply "taking feminism for granted", as has been the accusation of many "older" (read "real") feminists, especially since *The First Stone* was published, what then did, in fact, it mean we were doing?

In her book, Trioli answers some of these questions. *Talking Up* provides further reassurance that "feminism . . . in the hands of the next generation is alive and well, and as crucial as ever" (1996, p. 164). Trioli interviewed hundreds of young women and in using their stories, revealed their nous and strategic vision, their unsung community activism and their commitment to ideals of equity and justice. She paved the way for this collection of emerging voices. In giving the microphone to these women, we intend to dispel the idea that feminism is irrelevant in the 1990s, recently punitive or only about criticism. Instead, we want to illustrate that its principles and promotion, its goals and debates, are still part of many women's lives, including at their workplaces, in conversation, at home and in their relationships.

Equally important to the genesis of this anthology was Kathy Bail's *DIY Feminism* (1996). In some ways as a collection of articles by young women it is not dissimilar to this one, but for its premise that feminism was "about individual practice and taking on personal challenges" (1996, p. 16). It *sounds* very edgy. Let's face it, marketing feminism with groovy fonts, a funky layout and some pictures makes it palatable and digestible to a populist post-modern world. But it doesn't necessarily equate with social transformation, it isn't a call to action.

Multi vocal, savvy, with rock chicks, grunge and riot grrls: feminism pitched as sexy. *DIY* was so well-tuned for media take-up that despite the impressive range of contributors, it became a soundbite take-away. Its stumbling point is its marketing strength – truckloads of attitude. Are "fun and feisty" our only credentials these days? (1996, p. 9). If you are a woman with attitude, does this then make you a feminist? Much of do-it-yourself feminism just didn't wash with many of the women involved in this book. What if we can't do-it-ourselves? What if I can't? What if you can't? It is easy to assume that if we couldn't get on our modems, play in a band or be a bit wicked, then we wouldn't cut it. Bail sets up more politicised ideas of feminism as rigid, "dowdy, asexual" (1996, p. 5). With this stereotype entrenched once again, it is hardly surprising that she asserts that "women like me . . . are still less likely to make an issue of gender" (1996, p. 15).

We do not want to pit ourselves or these contributors against the DIY images, nor co-opt humourless, separatist stereotypes; but this anthology does not see feminism as either individualised, "disorganised" or even as much fun (1996, p. 15).

Many of the women who have contributed to this book found the writing process personally confronting, unlike anything they had written before. The brief required them to come face-to-face with their political commitments, emotional investments and their willingness to identify publicly as feminists. "What if I change my mind about this in five years?" some said. We are reminded of the reception of Naomi Wolf's second and third books, particularly *Fire with Fire* (1993) in which she was said to be refuting many of her views about female "victimhood" in *The Beauty Myth* (1990). So too Germaine Greer's visit to Melbourne in 1997 when, following her impassioned speech, questioning the nature of sexual liberation today, she was derided for changing her mind about women's sexual freedom, in spite of asserting that she still believed everything she wrote in *The Female Eunuch* (Greer: 1997, p. A17). These critical responses are underpinned by a belief that feminist behaviours are static, fixed and prescriptive. But if our political and social values are in any way informed by our experiences, then our philosophies, our ideas, our actions and how we live out our feminism must inevitably evolve.

A number of women, vocal about *The First Stone* and interested in this project did not submit a chapter as they were reluctant to expose themselves to the public baptism that printed ideas might engender. Others were excited about the book, but were also loath to be involved, not wanting to be derided at work, "ticked off by the old guard" or further embroiled within the politics of their university department. Such hesitancy is understandable. The importance of meditative and active silence in women's lives is examined by Cassandra Austin in this volume.

In November 1997, academic, Meaghan Morris told an audience at the Sydney Institute that her involvement in Jenna Mead's anthology *bodyjamming* elicited surprised responses from peers: "Good Lord! How did you get caught up in *that*?" they exclaimed. "Slowly, very slowly", Morris answered, driving home a wider point about the importance of time and reflection when dealing with such complex issues:

> *I prefer to think that genuine hesitation, rather than fear of abuse in the media, filled the silence of all those professional women who sympathised with the Ormond women in private but said nothing about it in public. I found the speed and virulence of media reactions to Garner's critics deeply shocking, given the evident complexity and, for those not closely involved, the obscurity of the Ormond events* (1998, p. 76).

To our surprise, along the way many of the contributors also asked "Who am I to say what feminism means?" Or "My idea of feminism is hardly 'in-yer-face'" or "But I'm not a member of a women's organisation." It is extraordinary that, at times, all of us worried that "feminism" would only grant us the right to speak under some, very particular and unspoken conditions. It seemed that we all looked for an authorising presence. But let's speculate for a moment and imagine what such validation might look like. Who would provide it? What would it authorise us to say? And most importantly, who would be "allowed" to speak?

As Misha Schubert points out, feminism is not, despite its impact, an institution. It has various institutional and legislative manifestations – such as democratic represent-ation, educational and employment opportunities, anti-discrimination, affirmative action and sexual harassment legislation, abortion rights, even no-fault divorce enshrined in the *Family Law Act* of 1975 – all thanks to extraordinary lobbying and campaigning by first- and second-wave feminists. Kate Lundy confesses to her late realisation ten years ago that without the *Sex Discrimination Act* of 1984, she would not have been given her first job on a building site. Her reflections on her responsibilities as a federal senator remind us that often our visions about a better world begin with issues that impact on our day-to-day lives. But with support and via active participation we can channel our concerns into social change.

These essays are not only about being young. Instead, they contain some new and some not-so-new ideas around feminist thinking and practice, they engage with a range of debates that are floating around the public and political arenas. They juxtapose personal experiences – some private and painful; some humorous and self-effacing – with rigorous positions about ways of being, thinking and treating each other. It is not trendy, there is no "new media", nor cutting edge to these ideas. Despite some recognisable motifs of post-modernist genres in a selection of the writings – definitional debate, historical revisionism, spoken language, and the use of pastiche and narrative – you will not read about the death of feminism here.

For many of the women in this anthology, college or university provided the formative moments for the growth of their feminist consciousness. Rosie Cooney tells stories that will resonate with anyone who has been involved with institutions or groups where men get drunk and messy and blokiness is the norm. Recalling her and her peers' experiences in a residential college, Cooney touches upon eating disorders, the power of the gang and the negotiations that attend the murky private/public space that one inhabits. Exposing the dangers of too much DIY, Debra Shulkes and Louisa Smith question how it is possible, in a supposedly post-feminist era, when we know all the rhetoric, the facts and the statistics about body shape and eating disorders, that we are still able to internalise our difference from an idealised norm of beauty. Undermining the attendant clichés of feminists as lesbians, Galina Laurie questions what it means to inhabit both of these identities and look like a girl.

The growth of Women's Studies and feminist revisionism within the Academy in the 1970s and 1980s has provided our generation of graduates – including interested men – the opportunity to read hidden histories, to develop ideas about gender relations, to explore feminist approaches to other disciplines, and consequently, to acquire new ways of seeing the world. Ingrid FitzGerald, in a discussion about gender, explores what legacies her university education provides her outside of tutorials. In a style that stands out for its lyricism, Emily Ballou connects her move from the United States to a personal and political awakening within feminist theory in Australia.

High-profile British feminist, Natasha Walter in *The New Feminism* (1998), extols a bright new future for feminism, based on increased access to material wealth and power, the reorganisation of homes and workplaces and support for women experiencing violence. Although Walter advocates an "unpicking of the tight link between the personal and the political" and implies the importance of public policy to force change, she acknowledges "that personal freedom can be aligned to political equality" (1998, pp. 4, 122). She paints a feminism which is inclusive and one which includes men. Jo Dyer reaches a similar conclusion highlighting the importance of dialogue when negotiating relationships between women and men, and suggesting that the bedroom is not necessarily the best place to be redressing political imbalance. And, Anita Harris' revisiting of heterosexual sex is more about self-honesty and self-rescue, than setting out prescriptive sexual behaviours and rules for feminists.

The title of this book suggests ideas about being young, and what that might mean. This stems from recent fascination with generational issues both inside and outside of feminism. However, grandmothers, mothers, lecturers, teachers, national and international feminist icons and writers – past and present – are some of the influential women acknowledged in these pages.

Relationships with our mothers – both actual and political is a frequent preoccupation throughout the book.

No contributor disputes that we can grow in experience and vision as we age, and that in ten years time some of us may be more moderate, or more radical. However, we do resent being typecast as unfeminist or anti-feminist, even post-feminist, by those who assert ownership (and imply invention) of the term. Herein lie the contentions that exist between older and younger women: that feminists are this, and not that. But to say "we are" should not mean "they aren't", nor that one is a greater truth than the other. Understanding, consciousness-raising and activism take many forms.

Louise D' Arcens, draws upon a medieval idea of sisterhood to imagine a new model for negotiating the complex and often fraught mother/daughter relationship within feminism. Finding connections in a more immediate heritage, Virginia McLean and Airlie Bussell trace the significance of their own mothers' and grandmothers' very different politics with the growth of their own feminisms. Ingrid McKenzie, concerned about the sidelining of youth generally from notions of social justice and from public forums, concludes "that there is room in feminism for all of us". Tara Gutman puts the case for more active female mentoring in the legal profession, arguing that the assistance and experience of older or more experienced female colleagues is invaluable for young women in the workplace.

It is commonplace to attribute feminism's divisiveness in Australia to the media – that most amorphous and evasive of creatures. It is endlessly frustrating to see that a "good story" is one based on conflict; and there's nothing better than two prominent feminists "having it out" in public. Maybe this explains much of the coverage of the United Nations Fourth World Conference on Women held in Beijing in 1995. The Conference was variously billed as a middle-aged talk-fest and an east-meets-west, rich-trammels-poor clash of absurd proportions. Several women included in this anthology attended the conference and the associated non-government forum. Suzette Mitchell provides us with an insider's view of the practicalities, political strength and inspiration associated with a gathering of this kind. She details the strategies used in forging alliances to fight for policy reform internationally and at home. Krysti Guest also touches on her experiences in Beijing as part of her growing awareness of feminism in global-economic terms. Guest's important structural critique rigorously puts our individual moments and voices into a larger perspective of privilege.

Often the best "hook" for young feminists looking for media profile is to trash the past, claiming our reinvention. Several contributors work in and with the media. Misha Shubert and Samantha Brazel bring a savvy and a thorough understanding of its methods and players to their writing and their different ways of living feminism in this environment. Vivienne Wynter, a media adviser and activist, refocuses the debate about sexism, racism and discrimination in media institutions and advertising. She encourages public engagement with the media and suggests alternative approaches to stories. Stephanie Gilbert highlights the media's inadequacy in portraying Aboriginal people's lives. She poses some crucial questions about personal beliefs and indigenous Australians, reminding us that politics must begin with respect for self-determination.

The strength of these chapters is their honesty, thoughtfulness and complexity, and their immunity to generalisation – it is impossible to summarise and difficult to condense. It is evident that youth is only a part of our identities: you will read about parliament and painted toes and everything in between. There is no one theme, nor a single common voice with which these young Australian women speak. As editors our task has been challenging and exciting throughout. It has focused our own feminist principles and tested our strength to stand up, be counted and speak. We are grateful to all those people who have listened to us talk about this for three years and believed that we could do it. Perhaps only editors say it is impossible to summarise their project, to reduce the whole; perhaps all editors only see the subtle differences between the breadth of ideas within the purview of their brief. We did, however, resist a written and generalised brief for some time, confident that commitments and beliefs have defining moments and that everybody has a story to tell. These are personal narratives, mini-memoirs explaining how feminism has changed our lives. Of course the eldest contributor is thirty-three years old and the youngest, seventeen, perhaps it is too early for memoirs. To support feminism, build on its legacies where they exist and envision a more just world is, in fact, where courage lies:

> *If only the whole gang of them hadn't been*
> *so afraid of life*
> *THE FIRST STONE*, HELEN GARNER: 1995, p. 222.

Learning Feminism

Feminist Glasses

Ingrid FitzGerald

> *I think it would be very odd if I wasn't a feminist, I don't*
> *know many black people who are take-it-or-leave-it on*
> *apartheid*
>
> M. EVARISTI: 1989, P. 180.

One of my favourite writers, Angela Carter, once said she was "in the business of putting new wine in old bottles – and preferably making the old bottles explode" (1983, pp. 69, 71). Carter's fiction mocks and undermines the conventions of masculinity and femininity. She points out what is obvious to many feminists – in order to create change we must start by reviewing and reframing where we are and where we have come from.

A feminist education has been invaluable to me. Like other critical perspectives, feminism provides ways of thinking through which I interpret and question society, culture and identity. Feminism has taught me the importance of thinking critically and sceptically about the status quo. It has become part of my equipment for living, the sewing kit I carry, the glasses I put on to examine what's happening around me. Feminism gives me the tools to understand and influence the status quo, as well as to imagine how society and relationships between men and women might be experienced differently.

My first exposure to feminist thinking occurred during my last two years of high school. Feminist teachers and subjects like "Women in the Media" gave me a taste of the politics and the theory feminism has to offer. I took Women's Studies as a major at the Australian National University (ANU) between 1989 and 1992. Like many other students, I found it the most intellectually stimulating and challenging subject I studied at university, in part because of its strong interdisciplinary approach.

Women's Studies first appeared in Australian universities in the early 1970s. The courses and programs arose out of the demand that women and gender issues be included in the curriculum. A strong cross-disciplinary approach and marginal status were early features. As Women's Studies evolved, it began to critique existing knowledges as based on the exclusion and denigration of women, and undertook the production of new knowledges, based on the positions, views and experiences of women (Sheridan: 1991, pp. 65-66).

While I was studying at the ANU, Women's Studies underwent a sea change, shifting from a sociological, historical and political focus to a more theoretical, post-modern approach. An essay I wrote in second year on women's spirituality and the return of the Goddess would have been unthinkable two years later. By the time I finished honours at the end of 1992, the program was strongly influenced by cultural studies, by an interest in texts such as advertising, film and literature, their representation of masculinity and femininity, and the ways that the reader or viewer relates to texts. Women's Studies also took up post-modern theories which deliberately unsettled the idea that our identity, as men and women, is fixed or stable. At the same time, we analysed the social and political effects of sexism and how we experience it in our everyday lives.

The feminist education I received was primarily academic, although not uninfluenced by feminist activism and popular feminist writing. As a result of this education, and my involvement in student activism, women's organis- ations and more recently in social policy, my feminism is eclectic – it refuses to specialise. It weaves together often contradictory perspectives: ecofeminist, socialist, liberal, riot grrl, post-modernist, to produce a complex braid of thinking and understanding which reflects the diversity of contemporary feminism. While diversity – of views, of politics, of strategies for change – is often bemoaned as dividing women, in my view it is one of feminism's strengths: the theoretical and political diversity offered by feminism mirrors the diversity among women.

The use of gender as a lens through which to understand our experience is one of the major contributions of contemporary feminist theory. The division between the categories "male" and "female" is a primary distinction in most societies. Social, economic and political power relations are based on this distinction. The term gender describes the division of male and female bodies into male and female classes, characterised by masculinity and femininity. The meanings attached to masculinity and femininity may change between historical periods and cultures, yet the distinction remains. While biologically sexed bodies are (we assume) universal, gender is differently constructed, understood and lived by individuals and communities. The implication is that our identities are not born but made, that femininity and masculinity are socially learned and constructed through technologies such as media, film, literature and medical, legal and political discourses (de Lauretis: 1987, pp. 2–3). Put another way, the body can be viewed as a surface for social inscription and meaning (Grosz: 1990, p. 63). The whole process of coming to be a person includes acceptance and internalisation of these inscriptions.

The racism debate, which has received so much public attention in Australia since 1996, illustrates how physical appearance can be used to mark individuals as members of a class and make them targets of hatred and abuse. Gender difference is reinforced in the same way. The dynamics of sexual harassment and sexual violence rest in part on the idea that a woman's dress or appearance, and even the female body itself are invitations to abuse. The dangerous cliché that certain clothes or behaviours invite invasion, is projected onto the female body, as though it were a blank screen. Our individual experiences, feelings and histories become meaningless as we step into the position of the universal female.

Unfortunately, as women we have been taught to internalise this assumption, policing our actions and appearance, even enacting our own punishment for "attracting" sexual violence. I recall reading in the paper in 1997 that a woman in Western Australia who had been raped by at least three men, had hanged herself rather than go to the police. The article suggested that she felt in some way responsible for the crime committed against her. Rather than seek justice, as victims of other violent crimes might have done, she took her own life. Her decision may have been based on the likelihood that the police would treat her as if she were to blame, that a court would probably do so, that her community was likely to judge her as having "asked for it", by the very fact of being a woman. Violent crime is often blamed on the victim, and not on those who are truly responsible; according to cultural norms responsibility for attracting male violence is part of what it means to be a woman.

When I walk down the street, towel over my shoulder as I head for the beach, I can't help being enraged when men whistle and shout at me from car windows. My "self", which has expanded in pleasure at the sun, the day, the things I am thinking about, is suddenly back in the box, caught in what Teresa de Lauretis calls the "wet silk dress" of femininity. Gender identity is indeed like a silk dress or grey suit which clings to us. Celebrate and stretch it as you like, it is still there. Femininity and masculinity attach to us, with meanings that stick. Being seen as male or female triggers a whole swag of associations whether we like it or not. There are, after all, only the *F* or *M* boxes to tick (de Lauretis: 1987, p. 12).

Gender identity is often taken for granted, seen as part of the "natural order", the way things are. In the same way that talk of "the family" assumes "the family" is universal and unchanging across time, gender is often seen as fixed, inevitable, so ordinary that we no longer see it. Gender becomes "unconscious"; we forget it is there. The paradox is that gender is at once visible and invisible: now you see it – of course women are responsible for sexual violence when they dress "inappropriately" – and now you don't – of course women are treated equally, what are you complaining about? While feminist glasses give me a clearer perspective on gender relations, at the same time, they make visible the ways in which gender is *hidden* from view.

I am very interested in the way that accounts of the social construction of gender have been recently side-lined. I detect a lack of interest about women's issues in contemporary public debate. I have yet to see a major newspaper analyse the combined impact on women's lives of the federal government's reforms to childcare, reproductive health services and industrial relations policy. At the same time, there has been a resurgence in the media of accounts which explain gender difference as biologically based. It may be that this trend arises from a re-emerging reluctance to recognise the effects of the gender distinction as socially constructed. Yet disavowal of the systemic effects of gender difference does not match up with a general recognition that economic inequality and racist attitudes are real and oppressive.

Liberal philosophy understands us as discrete autonomous individuals, able to act independently and achieve equally with others. This ideology informs the backlash against any critical theory which seeks to analyse the social and economic conditions that discriminate against people as groups. In the late-twentieth century, consumerism and liberal individualism have married to produce the peculiar idea that freedom is something we can purchase on the open market, rather than something we have to struggle for with others. According to this view, shored up by the media and by some readings of post-modern theory, being a woman doesn't matter. We are all individuals who can invent ourselves and do whatever we desire. We are bombarded with the idea that this is a post-feminist era. Assertions that discrimination and sexism are systemic forces are met with derision and accusations of victim consciousness and political correctness. In an interview in early 1997, Pru Goward, the head of the Office of Status of Women articulated this view. Goward, spokesperson for the national bureaucratic structure established to work for women's interests, defined the trajectory of contemporary women's politics as follows:

> We are finally seeing the left wing's domination of the Women's Movement weakened, which is why we're seeing young women rejecting victimhood. The Left has always used the image of the victim, the oppressed to advance its ideology. Young women today want to embrace competition, success, business . . . People are sick of the Thought Police (cited in Sheehan: 1997, p. 3).

Goward is not alone. I hear this view on the radio, on TV, among people I speak to about contemporary political culture. It is as if everyone was born into the middle class, with the same opportunities, as though some women and men no longer struggle to achieve success and juggle family and work. As though everyone's experience is the same, and if you have a tough time it's your own fault. It is as though it's too hard to think through the consequences of structural inequality, too hard to accept that there are some things over which we have limited control. This is a painful realisation, one we reach when we accept that violence, oppression and struggle are common in our society and in our world. So painful that it is no wonder we are willing to be seduced by the fiction that we exercise total freedom of choice in what we wear, how we act, and what we do. It's a grab bag of goodies, grrls.

Freedom, funnily enough, usually turns out to be the choice to buy an identity, to create through fashion, make-up, career role, a self which is supposedly unique and individual. But when I shop for clothes, I am presented with a series of uniforms: suits for the office in serious colours, little black dresses, velvet jumpers, hippy batik alternatives at Glebe markets and in Newtown, impossibly skinny fashion on Oxford Street. Gym shaped bodies greet me at Bondi clad in white t-shirts, blue or black jeans, sunglasses, high black sandals, and tans. My capacity to choose, to construct an identity through my appearance is constrained by what the market makes available and what the fashion and fitness gurus decree is acceptable. I have choice, indeed, but within limitations. If I choose not to accept a uniform, I am likely to be penalised, just as I was at school, by subtle or overt exclusion and derision. Nor can I endlessly re-shape my body to overcome the effects of ageing, or forestall death. Femininity is only a choice between uniforms selected by someone else who will pocket all the money.

Why do we desire to become that image we see in the windows of shops, in ads, on the overwhelming screen of the cinema? What explains its power over us? Why are we seduced by the fiction that we can choose? When we identify with an external, idealised image, we internalise it and we desire it. In so doing, we deny, at least temporarily, the absence, the gap between ourselves and the "image" we seek (Friedberg: 1990, p. 44). The idea that we are equal – can all access the same opportunities, can look like the skinny girls on the catwalk – is a total fiction, but it is one with enormous power, because it speaks to our longings and to our knowledge that life is messier than magazine ads.

The difference between a perspective that acknowledges the impact of gender difference and an approach which buys into the notion of individual freedom and autonomy is illustrated in the contrast between Evaristi's quote that heads this chapter and Kathy Bail's statement, (echoing Goward) that "feminism is largely about individual practice and taking on personal challenges rather than group identification" (1996, p. 16). While I agree with Bail and many of the contributors to *DIY Feminism* that each of us negotiates our own relationship to feminism, this approach also leaves me uneasy, because I am not yet ready to wholly disavow gender and its effects. Denying the gender distinction by buying into the idea that we are all individuals makes invisible the inequities imposed by gender relations. This erasure also undermines gender as a useful frame for understanding how we come to see and experience ourselves as men and women.

The reality of gender difference is disavowed by the assertion that this is a post-feminist era in which we are all individuals and can do whatever we like. The argument that we are "over all that" points the finger at those who talk about power relations, violence, inequality and rights, and names them as victims and whingers. We naturalise and legitimise inequality when we assume that our particular social and historical situation is inevitable, or when we deny that structural forces exist or are meaning-ful in our lives.

The feminist education I received exposed me to the possibility that identity is enacted, that we are masculine and feminine only as we perform these roles, that there is nothing intrinsic or essential about being a woman or a man. The suggestion that gender is a performance, that we are all "in drag", is exhilarating because it opens up a gap, enables a distance from the roles we play, so that we can understand them as learned and assumed. It allows us to begin to subvert and unsettle them. No longer need we see femininity and masculinity, maleness and femaleness as givens, but as masquerades, as performances, as a suit of clothes that we put on.

We know this experience, dressing up, putting it on, faking it, the work suit or cocktail dress. This playfulness is obvious in the carnival that is the Sydney Gay and Lesbian Mardi Gras, where gender roles and the idea of masculinity and femininity are bent out of shape, parodied, and satirised. Gender parody is evident whenever masculinity and femininity are performed to excess, excess which reveals their "unnaturalness". I think of the hypermasculinity of Rambo, the hyperfemininity of woman as bitch or victim in *Melrose Place*, and of Madonna as Material Girl. All these fictions ridicule the inevitability of gender roles by exposing the fantasies that underpin them – perfect, invincible male bodies, flawlessly made up, Barbie-doll female bodies.

I struggle with identifying these images as simply fictional, however, because talking about gender as a social construct or performance can quickly lead to the suggestion that gender is somehow not real. If masculinity and femininity are seen as mutable, then surely we can just decide to change them and create something different?

It's here that post-modern theory and the liberal individual as consumer collide. Back in the shopping mall again, I am cautious. I know that gender does matter, that it is *material*. Very real inequities and oppressions continue to be based on the distinction. For example, critical analysis of assumptions about what it means to be a woman or a wife assist us to understand the prevalence of domestic violence. According to a study conducted in late 1996 by Women's Safety Australia, 1.3 million Australian women have suffered a partner's physical violence. Sixty-five per cent of these women were aged between eighteen and thirty-four (Bernoth: 1997, p. 7). The same young women that are sold the myth that we are living in a post-feminist era, with the fantasy of unlimited choice and freedom, are those contending with the destructive effects of gender roles in their relationships.

It's a commonplace to say that women are not all the same, nor are we discrete individuals. If we reject an analysis of how gender constructs us, and accept the individualist myth of plastic bodies and identities that can be endlessly reshaped and reformed (for a price) we are, like Jeannie of the TV show, eternally trapped inside the bottle.

Ultimately, we are all products of our social and cultural circumstances. While we may deny this, we can't escape it. We can never be totally outside ideology. However, feminism offers us a double vision. Exposing the social construction of gender creates a distance, a gap. This gap enables us to take up a position which is at once "inside and outside the ideology of gender and conscious of being so" (de Lauretis: 1987, p. 10). We look though the glasses, we look over the top of them, we see things differently. We have a perspective from which to start to shift things, to create what Angela Carter described as "new wine".

For me, feminist accounts of gender difference provide a lens, a set of glasses through which femininity and masculinity can be viewed as constructs which shape and frame our experience. Feminism is not a single ideology, nor does it provide a complete and cohesive view of the world. Rather, it offers a perspective which informs my understanding of how we come to be who we are. Glasses are only an instrument, a tool, which enable me to see more clearly. The gender lens is undoubtedly useful, yet just as feminism is shifting and mutable, these glasses are not a fixture. That's what I like about them, that I can put them on and take them off, shifting my perspective each time. A feminist education provided me with these glasses. I don't see the world the same way I did before I acquired them and I'm glad.

How to Be a Woman: Things I Learned in College

Rosie Cooney

Within venerable walls of sun drenched sandstone, shabby, streaked, grey, poured-concrete, or monolithic red brick, young men and women throughout the country live in a unique form of close confinement. They sleep in rows of beds mere metres apart; eat every meal communally; play sport; drink; dance and study together. These institutions are wholly voluntary, avowedly beneficial and, for thousands, form the basis of university social lives and relationships. This is a hidden world, the world apart, of university colleges.

Learning

College turned me into a feminist
Mary Rose, 24.

In their late teens, women and men reach the end of over
a decade of formal schooling; a world bound by the rules
and dictates of teachers and parents; disciplined by
timetables, curfews, bells and homework. They move on to
university – many into residential colleges – and the world
changes. For many, colleges are a first taste of freedom, a
welcome release. Virtually all supervision has ceased –
alcohol, friends and time are all free and abundant. A new
period of learning begins. Outside is university, and formal
education in disciplines and professions. Inside, within the
sheltering walls of colleges, a different process begins. Men
and women are trained in the expectations of the social
world. They learn what forms of behaviour are acceptable,
censured, and rewarded. They learn their sex: the responses
expected from them, the appearance required and the
forms and modes of relationships considered acceptable
and normal.

The lessons colleges teach, however, form a primer of
regressive and destructive sexual politics. In these enclaves a
culture flourishes in which the worst excesses of Australian
macho masculinity reign free and unfettered. Women slot,
awkwardly, into a boys' own playground of beer, mateship
and blatant objectification of women. In colleges women
live enmeshed by a culture of "laddishness". They are
defined by it, judged by it, and they judge themselves by it.

In college, I formed some of my strongest friendships,
had a lot of fun, grew up a little and learned a great deal.
However, I was also angry, frustrated, hurt and disgusted.

This chapter is a personal account of three years in college, drawn from my own and others' experiences. It is an attempt to describe and explain the impact of living in an environment which systematically and relentlessly undermines and devalues women.

In this so-called post-feminist age, the need to understand the way in which the marginal status of women is created and reproduced is greater than ever. Many feminists concentrate on the tangible economic and material disadvantages of women. Many forms of feminism seek to identify an authentic female subjectivity; one which is not defined by, or in opposition to men. To create a feminism that addresses the lived experience of young women – to create the space for women to emerge as autonomous and powerful subjects – we need to understand the ways in which society's cultures and institutions attack and degrade their experience and sense of self-worth.

In the Hothouse

> There were whole weeks when I did not leave college, except to play sport. There were probably months when I didn't leave campus, except to frequent local drinking holes, and even this was always with a bunch of college friends
>
> JESSICA, 19.

Colleges are worlds distinguished by their invisibility. Their arcane rites and rituals occur in a parallel universe largely unseen and unreported, even to the broader campus population. Odd glimpses of college life pop up in student publications, but little filters through to the mainstream. This insulation has several effects. Isolation shields these institutions from the changes in the rest of society. Stepping into college is a cogent reminder of a world before feminism. Typically, college cultures are woefully divorced from progressions in thought and behaviour outside their walls. This means that within colleges, the same set of retrograde behaviour and attitudes can be reproduced almost infinitely, for generations. As each crop of new students arrives, they absorb the language, habits and attitudes of the old and continue the tradition by passing them along to their successors.

Perhaps more importantly, the insulation of colleges forbids critical assessment. For me college became, for a time, the whole world. My entire social life was lived, metaphorically and very nearly literally, within its confines. College activities – sport, bar nights, debating, endless teas and coffees – ate up every waking moment, leaving scant space for objective reflection. This kind of intense involvement prescribed not only my movements but also my mind. Because it was impossible to compare my life with others, I accepted the status quo with little questioning. It is alarmingly easy to find atrocious behaviour utterly natural when not exposed to anything different. Later, when talking about college to those who had never gone through it, I realised how bizarre and downright embarrassing much of college life seemed from the outside. But at the time I, like most others, had too little distance and too little opportunity for comparison.

Colleges exist in a vacuum in which objectivity is impossible. With their close confines, their concentration of activities, and insulation from the outside, types of people and forms of behaviour that would shrivel and die under the cold light of social scrutiny are encouraged, and flourish.

Hell Men and Other Peculiar Creatures

Best years of my life
STEVEN, 25.

Throughout Australian culture, there runs a distinct strain
of laddish yob: the boozy, blokey, "show us yer tits" model
of masculinity. In public, under pressure from feminists and
others who find it embarrassing, this type is becoming rarer,
even endangered. In the sheltering and congenial college
hothouse, however, a celebrated, magnified version thrives.

College is relentlessly blokey. From the first day of
Orientation Week, when the boys stand around in groups,
eyeing first-year girls, drooling and "spading", "the lads"
dominate the social atmosphere. And these are the hard-
drinking, rugby-playing, backbone-of-the-college types.
One herd in my own college was fond of calling themselves
the "hell men". They could pull chicks, sink lager, achieve
perfect fifty-one per cent scores in exams, and displayed
every sign of being proud of this. And these were not
aberrant fringe creatures. In terms of setting the atmosphere
at social events and occasions, they were probably the
most influential group in college. College events were tests
of strength and occasions for displays of prowess: "Now,
which one of us big strong lads can drink the most beer and
crack onto the most first-year women?" It was a glorious
only-just-post-adolescent fantasy, of mates, beer and chicks.

Drinking is a predictably conspicuous feature of college
life. Indeed, for many, I am sure it remains the strongest
and fondest memory. I was pressed into service on my first
day, downing pints in a boat race. The year progressed in
a welter of more beer, ever more esoteric drinking games
and a lurid variety of liquids in shot glasses. For many,

virtually every college event – barbecue, ball, quiz night, formal dinner – revolves around attaining thorough and rapid obliteration. It is common for people to beat a quick retreat for a speedy regurgitation, then rejoin the fray with undimmed enthusiasm. One particular drinking game is played with garbage bins strategically placed around the room, for any sudden "overflow". The morning after, the story telling starts: who drank what, how drunk they were, who "hooked in" with whom, and what happened on the way home.

Drinking is hardly an exclusively male activity, and while men and women may make up college students in comparable numbers, men overwhelmingly dominate the tone and atmosphere of colleges. Although women are certainly a part of this scene, and active in it, they are less influential in determining social norms and passing judgment on behaviour. In college, the atmosphere is set by the loudest voices, which are typically male. Women who speak up risk social condemnation, or being disliked and thought unattractive – all harsh penalties in a confined social world. Women avoid being publicly offensive, something for which many of the men seem to feel little aversion. The result is a situation in which the loudest of the lads determines standards of behaviour and women, in general, go along with them, or are ruthlessly silenced.

Playing Along

Everything you did or said was scrutinised, gossiped about, picked to bits. There was a rigid code of what was acceptable. Anything else was seen as vaguely antisocial or just plain weird. I think I'm pretty normal, but I was constantly called weird in college

KAREN, 22.

College life holds out a promise: the promise of acceptance, of belonging, of being part. It draws in people who are unsure about where they fit in, who they want to be, and presents them with a ready-made identity and group membership. The powerful traditions of college life offer a template for behaviour, and proximity creates a ready-made circle of friends. The lure of group membership inculcates the fierce and often completely unfounded loyalties that spring up among college neophytes, and remains with those who do not find disenchantment. A powerful myth of a sheltering and protective family emerges. When my class of first-years turned up, we were assured by the older boys that college was indeed "one big happy family"; they would protect and shelter our young and vulnerable selves. We had arrived in a utopian community of big brothers and little sisters. Their somewhat predatory intentions later became clearer, but at the time we believed it, and I think they believed it too. Collectively, we were immersed in the warm glow of belonging.

The appeal of the group and a sense of loyalty induces a wholesale adoption of group standards of behaviour. In my college the prevailing culture had an alarming ability to draw people in and model them into carbon copies of each other. As a second-year, I realised that boys who had started as thoughtful individuals had been transformed into the new crop of unimproved good ol' boys, mouthing the same lines, the same tired jokes, their own personae dissolved in the cult of the college hero. Little is demanded of those who aspire to acceptance: say the right things, act the right way, and you can join the embrace of the group. For the men, acceptance means, more or less, being easygoing. This requires that they are politically conservative and sporty; place social and college life ahead of academic pursuits; and talk about women with a laundry-list style of discourse: "Good body but a face like a horse." "Nice tits but she's got a big bum." For women, the most valuable quality was cuteness, with the requisite docility. It was also important to be sociable and engaging; intelligent, although neither terribly thoughtful nor intellectually threatening; and sexually appealing, while always retaining a delicate veneer of sexual reticence.

For those who are too different, too uncompromising or too clever, the social penalties can make life miserable. One friend found the boys obnoxious, immature and uninteresting, and while polite by nature made little attempt to hide her opinion. She was the object of continual jibes and small taunts: "Been off sharpening your knives, Kate?" accompanied by a performance of a Macbeth-like stabbing of the air in front of her. She left the college and the city after a year, having comprehensively failed her exams and developed a well-founded loathing of institutions.

The Ratings Game

> She was my best friend in college. I lived virtually next door to her for two years. I never knew that she was seriously bulimic the whole time. I was having fun while she was puking her guts up after every meal
>
> MICHELLE, 22.

Women are ruthlessly objectified in the boozy, cheery atmosphere of colleges; reduced to a one-dimensional reflection of male desire. In what amounts to an over-sized dorm room, women are exposed to several-hundred critical, assessing eyes. They experience continual comment on their appearance and understand that their personal charms will be dissected and assessed at leisure. Classified according to a rigid index of desirability, women learn very quickly to which category they have been allotted. This regime of scrutiny breeds women who are paranoid about their looks and weight; who view themselves and assess their self-worth through the eyes of others; and are acutely sensitive to criticism on their appearance; obsessive about eating, dieting and comparing themselves to others.

In my college, little respect was shown to individual sensitivities. Assessment of women was public, face-to-face and acceptable as an ordinary form of conversation. Across the dining tables, in the course of blithe, convivial banter, girls were told they had "a hairy face" or "saggy tits". The appropriate response was a witty one-liner and feigned unconcern. The effect, however, was to underline to women the tenuous nature of their hold on power: they could be so easily undermined, subjected to public humiliation, and reduced to a physical trait. And they literally were commented on by all: the dissection could be blatant to the point of ridiculous. Boys in my own college distributed and filled out an elaborate written survey. Women were rated in categories such as "face" or "body"; with sub-categories such as "best tits" and "most toned". The results of this survey were read out to a packed and carousing hall, to much public hilarity and a great deal of private trauma. Far from aberrant or isolated, this sort of gratuitous objectification forms the very backbone of college culture.

Against this background, it is little wonder that eating disorders are widespread in colleges. While I am aware of no statistics on their incidence in these institutions, I am still, several years on, learning of friends or acquaintances that were bulimic or anorexic. Intimately connected to these excesses of anxiety is the unremitting emphasis on women's bodies by the men with whom they live. The bulimic walks in to the canteen to be told she has a fat bum, gorges on chocolate and throws it up in an orgy of despair and self-loathing. The anorexic is praised for her initial loss of weight, and redoubles her efforts in search of approval. The overweight girl is dismissed as sexually invisible and therefore socially irrelevant. Usually eating disorders are painful, private secrets that may be endured without being shared for many years. Sometimes they become quasi-public: in one neighbouring college an after-dinner chuck almost became a social event. Whatever their nature, they are symptoms of severely eroded self-esteem and distorted conceptions of self-worth, fostered by an environment that values neither.

Female desirability is of a fragile and sacrificial nature in this milieu. Women's social worth is conditional on male approval. Female sexuality is depressingly reactive – an enforced reflection by women of what men want or expect from them. Genuine female sensuality or sexuality is completely absent from college life: absent from the customs, the language, and the values of the dominant culture.

The tenure of a woman's desirability is marked by the length of male interest: as first-years arrive – posing tantalising new opportunities and interests – last year's models are shunted aside and ignored. Women soon lose their wide-eyed innocence and with it their faith in their new-found family. The boys who, the previous year, professed their eternal friendship, switched their attentions and "protective" intentions to the newly arrived freshers. And so "second-year-girl syndrome" arises – a common feeling amongst later-year women, that they no longer have a place in college. This means depression or an enduring bitterness for some women. Others quickly realise the fickleness of much of college life, and move on or move out. Colleges frequently have problems retaining older female students. This means the older students who are influential in setting the atmosphere and tone of college are predominantly male, and each year as the new first-years arrive, the cycle rolls on.

Notching the Bedpost

I used to watch them at bar nights. The boys would encourage the girls, especially the first-years, to get really, really drunk. Then they'd just move in and pick out one to take up to their room

KATRINA, 22.

Women arriving at college are fresh out of school and often extremely naive. Plucked from their support systems of family and friends, they are newcomers in a scene where they do not know the possibilities or understand the rules; frequently they are acutely vulnerable. On the first day I arrived at college, I realised the first-year girls were the focus of attention, or the focus for one group at least. The attention was flattering and fascinating. They painted a beguiling picture of the joys of college life; the eternal friendships that awaited us; their own vital role as our protectors and guides; the caring, sharing, happy family we had just joined. A pervasive element of point scoring, and a manly quest to bed the newcomers ran through this rhetoric. One friend was horrified to learn not only was she awarded "most bonkable", but that a case of beer was riding on her head, a prize for the triumphant victor. Adding to her disillusionment was the realisation that the quest had been played out among her new found "friends".

Sexual harassment in college is not a culpable aberration, but a completely unremarkable fact of life. Date or acquaintance rape is frequent and uncondemned. The "fuck-a-fresher" syndrome – older boys viewing first-years as easy sexual targets – is a tableau repeated with various levels of subtlety year after year. Rebecca's story illustrates a typical college scenario. In her first week, straight from school, naive and a virgin, two boys she had met during the week dropped by her room for a chat, and one stayed on talking. She was impressed by his sensitive, liberal line of discussion, and his avowed understanding of feminist issues. He extolled the virtues of affirmative action and his sympathy for the vulnerability of first-year women. Suitably overcome by his outright snagishness, they fell into a clinch. She had no wish to sleep with him, and made this clear. His carefully wrought new found sensitivity, however, appeared mysteriously to evaporate. He persisted, refusing to take her repeated "no" for an answer. As she put it: "It got to the point where it was almost coercion. It wasn't until I threatened to scream and wake up the entire corridor that he finally stopped."

This banal scenario is repeated in various forms over and over in college life. Women who are less confident, easily overwhelmed, or who fear social penalties if they refuse, often end up having sex when they do not want to, and in situations where they are uncomfortable. Some recent commentators, feminist and otherwise, have decried the contemporary emphasis on acquaintance rape and sexual harassment, advocating a return to time-honoured female tactics of face slapping and polite-but-firm refusals. In many typical college scenarios, these would be manifestly ineffective. More importantly, those who advocate a bit of hefty knee action ignore how simply inexperienced and unsure of themselves many women are when they begin university. They are not confident, they are anxious about being alienated or ostracised in this new society and they know everything that happens will be later conveyed to the coterie of lads. Many have simply not yet realised that sex looms large in the minds and glands of their new friends. They might not speak out because they understand the potential repercussions. Alternatively, they may have not yet realised that they can speak out.

Despite this pressure, a double standard that penalises and condemns women's sexuality while glorifying men's is a prominent feature of college life. In my college, the mere accumulation of sexual "conquests" was a confirmation of male status. One of the aforementioned "hell men" boasted of his target of fifty by his twenty-first birthday; a goal which, rumour has it, he reached.

Each year the student body organised a public prize-giving ceremony, for male and female "sluts of the year". A roomful of cheering, yelling students applaud the winners. The male winner is invariably drawn from the most prominent of the various crowds, part of the accepted social core of college life. He is a virtual hero, and his win is hailed with slaps on the back and some covert envy. The girl, however, is typically less popular and her award is a cause for hilarity rather than adulation. While she may accept her award with head held high, she is followed by sniggering and derisive laughter. She has become material for gossip and condemnation and an "easy lay".

Rosie Cooney

Learning Revisited

*Many are scarred for life. Many wake up and grow
up to be good feminists*

Kate, 23.

This is not a victim story. The upshot of going through the college system is hugely variable, and by no means uniformly negative. Some women leave carrying insecurities, trauma and painful emotional baggage. Others are effectively moulded into shape; following the line of least resistance, internalising and conforming to the values and attitudes of the college environment. Still others, however, experience college life as a wake-up call that alerts them to the sexual politics that shape women's lives. It sensitises them to the use and abuse of male power. For me, it took a year or so before frothy first-year merriment turned into exasperation and irritation. While college remains a memory of happiness and challenges, its darker side led directly to my own awareness of and engagement with feminism.

Ultimately, both men and women are caught in the stagnant cultural cycle of college life. Long term, perhaps men have even more to lose, because they graduate from university unaware of the artificial nature of college culture. Within several years, women friends have moved on, whereas the men, the "lads", are little changed: making the same jokes, drinking with the same crowd, reminiscing on the glory days of college life. It seems tertiary education required little from them except continuing a great Australian tradition of boozy, unreflective masculinity.

Change to this environment would involve some delicate questions of blame and responsibility. I hesitate to blame individual boys for the ills sustained by women in college. In my experience, many of the boys were undeniably immature and insensitive; prone to mindless excess and unthinking cruelty. They are, however, encouraged in that disposition by the reigning orthodoxy and they receive no indication that something more thoughtful is required of them. College administrators are often to blame for putting the reputation of their college ahead of the well-being of their students. While at university, I wrote an article about the "fuck-a-fresher" syndrome for the student newspaper, drawing on interviews and conversations with former students. At one college, from which several interviewees were drawn, the principal was anxious to allay first-years' anxiety, and announced to all that "it doesn't happen here". In the same college, two days later, I spoke to a fourth-year girl who said quietly, out of the earshot of the throng, that she had watched it happen year after year. Administrators of colleges fail their students, and society at large, if they lack the perspicacity to face the problems that exist, and the courage to address them.

This chapter reflects my own experience, and while it will not be true for all, or of all institutions, I am confident it reflects the experience of many. Colleges are important institutions. They take people at a particularly impress-ionable stage of life, determine in large the shape of their entire university experience and instil values or attit-udes which remain in place for life. Currently, they typically remain isolated backwaters of retrograde chauvinism, educating women and men in the manners and mores of a sexist status quo.

Like a Corporate Virgin

Tara Gutman

The next wave of women . . . know instinctively that in their ambitious working lives their gender is still an issue, but they have largely been brought up in an environment where passionate feminism is not only unfashionable it is unattractive

VIRGINIA TRIOLI: 1996, P. 61.

I wasn't born a pilot or a lawyer. I have become these. Nor was I born a feminist. I have become one. Unlike the former, which are the result of specific training, it is hard to say how, or even when, I became a feminist. I can, however, identify times when I have taken stock of my principles; moments of clarity where I can see the impact and influence of other women – role models and mentors – on my personal and professional development. Not everyone seeks out role models. As an only child, I looked because I wanted to know how to bridge the gap between myself as a teenager and the many older people around me.

I think of my mother as a capable person. She spent her early twenties studying archaeology in Burmese jungles before writing her PhD and raising me. As an educated woman and independent thinker, she was part of a generation of babyboomer women who were emotionally and financially self-sufficient enough to leave their marriages. We spent part of my childhood at arm's length. Today I admire her, we are close and share many common interests; she continues to have a stimulating professional life, a generous sense of humour and more *joie de vivre* than a paragraph can do justice. But perhaps because we were not close when I was an adolescent, hers has not been an example I have consciously followed. In fact, I spent a great deal of time trying not to emulate her: when many friends took up smoking, I adamantly refused, mainly for fear of having something in common with my mother.

In my teens, I had a magnificent role model in my grandmother with whom I lived. After half a century of marriage to a stern European husband who forbad her from wearing make up or earrings and from leaving the house in short sleeves, she arrived in Australia for the first time in her life, a widow aged eight-seven. Immediately she arrived she adorned herself with clip-on earrings and took up smoking to see what the fuss was about. In her mid-nineties she discovered plush velour leisure suits which did away with the need to iron. She took pleasure from doing my French homework (how could I argue?), watched foreign soapies, test drove the latest hearing aids and brewed the strongest coffee; she grew competition standard geraniums and preferred Lindt chocolate, thank you anyway. She died at 102, leaving me with a strong sense of old age being about contentment and generosity, and the freedom to indulge oneself and others. I wondered what terrain I would traverse in the long gap between my adventurous early teens and peaceful old age.

I was a lazy and unsophisticated university student when I learned that "same" does not mean "equal". It was in a feminist legal studies class, much of which went over my head because I hadn't kept up with the prescribed reading. I spent most of my time in this class wondering about my peer's private lives. Did they actually reconcile all this theory within themselves and live by its principles? Did it affect the clothes they wore, and the chores they did or didn't do at home? How would they bring up their sons and daughters? The lecturer explained that treating everyone equally did not mean that each would benefit equally, and that equality of distribution can amount to inequality of result. She argued that some had less to start with and so needed different treatment to achieve the same outcome. Affirmative action, positive discrimination, redressing an imbalance – call it what you will – it was starting to make sense. The lecturer was so rigorous and passionate about the subject that, at the beginning of the course, most of the class assumed she was a dyke. It was only at the end of the semester when most students' views had developed considerably, that we realised that homosexuality was not a prerequisite to being an articulate feminist. No longer remotely curious about her sexuality, I saw in her qualities I wanted to emulate.

At that moment I was given a lens through which to see more than ever before. I read the literature, sometimes uncritically, argued and made assertions of sexism. When author Susan Brownmiller wrote that the power imbalance between the sexes is so great that all sex was necessarily rape,[1] I announced to my parents that I would be conscientiously celibate, possibly forever, but at least until I worked out whether Brownmiller was right. I put the *f* word in my pocket and I was not afraid to use it.

I met a different kind of role model while watching *Countdown* on a Sunday night in the mid-eighties. My mother announced that dinner was nearly ready; would I set the table? Not now. I was transfixed. Madonna appeared in a midriff top, legwarmers and liquid eyeliner. Our first meeting was during the "Holiday" film clip. I say meeting because we do kind of know each other, although it is true we have never actually met. She knew her audience, I knew what I read in *TV Week*, who she was seen with, whose clothes she wore, the market she stalked. There is a degree of reciprocity there if you look.

Madonna was a trail blazer. Men were her back-up dancers, her playthings and we never saw any sign of a band. It was all about her. "Holiday" was a product of the eighties with no notable musical significance other than as a vehicle for a performer who would propose a new paradigm of sexual power. A short time later her film clip for "Burning Up" showed her writhing around in the middle of a road. She was instantly sexual. She sang about urgent desires rather than goosebumps or waiting from nine to five for her baby's train to arrive home. She was powerful and unruly. As the song proclaimed "I'm not the same/ I have no shame/ I'm on fire." At last someone to embody the paradox: Madonna became a symbol of power at the same time as being sexy. Capitalising on her own

---

1   (1976). *Against Our Will.*

body, she was both feminine and feminist. The same could not be said of many other women in the public eye at the time.

Live at the Sydney Cricket Ground, Madonna strutted around with a riding crop before sliding down a fireman's pole in lingerie, dancing provocatively with women and simulating masturbation to the point of orgasm. The total package was daring for the mainstream audience. I thought of my mother and grandmother. They probably would have found it excessive and distasteful respectively, whereas I was exhilarated – not because the show shocked me but because it was possible: sexual liberation had come a long way.

Girls could do anything. Supposedly. Parents and teachers had always said so. But Madonna showed me so. Her public performance provided irrefutable evidence. Madonna took up the mantle for a generation who required that ideas about sexual self-sufficiency be re-invented in our times. Although I didn't exactly want to be her, I took satisfaction from the fact that she could do what she was doing. But given that even our feminist mothers rarely let us see into their bedrooms, we never quite knew how to translate the "go girl" idea into the private zone. My mother's generation won the right to equal pay, fought for the means to control their fertility and acknowledged that sex could be without commitment. As a result women were more able, as men had always been, to quarantine emotional behaviour from sexual behaviour. Post sexual revolution, these ideas have been absorbed into our collective consciousness. Madonna confirmed all the implied messages that I was receiving. Furthermore, there was something reassuring about her brazen, blatant, unsubtle delivery. She publicly exploited taboo issues which were still, or once again, considered private. I understood this new, self-appointed high priestess of popular culture to say that women can overtly demand the highest levels of commitment and sexual satisfaction; and, that women are responsible for their own happiness, well-being and sexual health. The AIDS caveat hadn't tempered previous generations' activities.

I only began to doubt my semi-conscious belief that "everything would fall into place" when, following graduation from law school, I landed a job in a large Sydney commercial law practice. At this point, there was not a lot Madonna or my grandmother would be able to do for me. They had not worked in law firms, where eighty per cent of the bosses are men and where young women mince around in navy and black looking immaculate and busy, and not rocking the boat. There are few female faces in the legal world's hall of fame. Women presently make up over fifty per cent of students in law faculties and there is an expectation that over time these women will find their way to the top ranks of the profession. But in the interim there exists a hiatus, not just because of the time lag between women's access to education and the time it takes to reach the upper rungs. Although equal numbers of women and men secure a toehold at the bottom of the profession, the number of women dwindles as you glance up the ladder.

On my first day of work at the firm, I took an elevator to the thirty-second floor and looked around to find that of the seventy-five partners in the Sydney office only fifteen were women. I asked a male partner to explain this. His answer was that the ratio had very little to do with gender and more to do with academic results and training. Moreover, he said, it was changing extremely quickly. The qualification seemed strange given that half the junior solicitors were female. By senior associate level, there were markedly fewer women because "reproduction was an impediment". Four years later, sixteen of the seventy-one partners in the firm's Sydney office are women. So much for rapid change. Assuming this rate of increase is maintained, it will be 2040 before fifty per cent of partners in the firm are women. And as it turns out a twenty per cent female partner rate is actually regarded as exemplary among the profession; one of Sydney's large firms currently only has five per cent of women with partnerships.

My concern was that in the transition from student culture to corporate culture, from overplayed confidence to appropriate workplace deference, I found a gaping black hole. Many women lose the edge they may have had over their male classmates when they set foot in law firms. At school I was judged by my achievement: good marks were one sign of success. At the University of New South Wales, the law school used a Socratic, interactive teaching method, and success was a composite of a student's ability to speak up in class and their marks in assignments. By contrast, in a law firm accomplishments played second fiddle to one's ability to fit into the system.

Young lawyers compete in the workplace making an effort to be noticed and fast tracked. If you are one of dozens, it is easy to get lost and appear busy when in fact you are stagnating. As a new lawyer, I was made to feel insecure about my abilities. Would I come up with the right answers fast enough and present them in the right way?

These are coveted positions, and you are expected both to tread lightly and make a big splash. In an environment where there is so much scope for things to go wrong, signs from above are invaluable. Assistance of this kind may come from role models whose behaviour we seek to emulate, or from mentors who take an active, more personal interest in an individual and her career. Mentors do not prescribe a mode of behaviour, rather they suggest ways of tailoring institutional practices to your needs and personality.

The legal profession is inherently conducive to mentoring, which can help young people to become well connected – critical to achieving any reasonable level of success. Private school networks, university colleges, family ties, sporting connections and religion are some of the traditional coteries which have generated the patronage of new lawyers by older ones. Legal culture today remains simultaneously hierarchical and male: we bow to acknow-ledge the superiority of judges who sit on high thrones and hand down judgements. Letters to law firms are addressed to "Messieurs XYZ" regardless of the recipient's gender; judges refer to each other as "brethren"; the collective noun describing all male and female lawyers is the legal "fraternity". Women are expected to wear skirts in most offices most of the time but, at the very least, when appearing in court. This unwritten rule exists despite antidiscrim-ination legislation introduced over a decade ago. The rules governing appearance require more of women: while men must wear suits and generally be clean shaven, women have to address the whole catastrophe – nails, stockings, heels, make-up, a variety of smart, fetching, but not too appealing, outfits in a range of corporate colours.

Mentors provide an alternative to operating in isolation which, in my experience, is often cited as one of the reasons women leave these organisations, along with lack of support or positive feedback. They provide clues about protocol in an environment where everyone is expected to act within particular boundaries. Formalised mentor systems would, I believe, be beneficial to all junior staff, but most particularly to young women. But there is no reason why a woman's mentor need be female. Men can be equally inspiring, compelling figures, although there may be advantages in speaking to a woman if you are contending with gender issues in a workplace. I have worked closely, happily and productively with a number of men who have given me useful feedback on my work and set fine examples. But more often than not, it is impressive women that I want to emulate. Despite the likelihood that women will be effective communicators in a workplace, there is no guarantee that a woman will be a good mentor. Not everyone is capable of, or interested in, pointing juniors in the right direction. Not everything can be taught – some lessons are yours to learn alone – but by observing workplace behaviours and drawing from the experience of others, young players are minimising their chances of falling into traps.

I encountered my first mentor while working as a paralegal in a close-knit team of litigators preparing for a major media case. I arrived wearing a suit awkwardly, and in special new stockings that were supposed to stay up themselves without suspenders but unfortunately didn't. I had practised wearing high heels around the house for a day. I was assigned to a supervising lawyer who was generous with her time and expertise. Unlike most of the women in the firm, she wore low-heeled shoes and trousers rather than skirts. Unlike most of the lawyers, she also brought her "self" to work: her wit and vitality. She demonstrated that it was not necessary to feign a personality bypass in order to be productive and highly regarded. Mundane tasks became interesting and worthwhile when she animatedly explained how they would be used in court during the trial. Casual anecdotes about her experiences as a junior bridged a gap between where I was and where I might end up. I had been mistaken in my assumption that to conform to the recipe for a good woman lawyer would be a sign of weakness: it pays to mix all the requisite ingredients in a way that is your own. There is room to move, to spice up the recipe. She taught me that conformity becomes power when you do it in a fashion that suits you.

While there appears to be consensus among women in the legal profession regarding matters of equal pay, the benefits of part-time positions, parental leave, or carrying condoms in handbags, women lawyers are less willing to call themselves feminist and are sometimes reticent to encourage other women. Often, being a feminist has come to mean taking care of yourself to the exclusion of others. Sisters doin' it *only* for themselves without a thought for other sisters are not playing a part in a feminist community. However, until women bring their gender to the office, it is likely that the notion of the male lawyer as the norm will remain. This means taking seriously a range of matters, including childcare, paid maternity and paternity leave and guarding against salary discrimination.

At my next job in another major commercial law firm, I was told by a senior associate that I wasn't doing myself any favours by overplaying "the female thing". He suggested

I approach the law more like a lawyer and less like a woman. His implication was worrying: that being a lawyer means not being a woman; that the two are not compatible; that being a good lawyer is about being unfemale, or even that lawyerliness is inherently male. Yet these binaries are false and unhelpful. Women are encouraged to down play their gender and, ideally, to make it invisible. Furthermore, women who argue that they have achieved partnership simply because of their professional skills fail to explain why the gender imbalance in law firms is so shocking. There is no evidence which suggests that women are less skilled at studying or practising law. That firm, the most gender equitable of Sydney's biggest six at the time of writing, currently has twenty female partners out of eighty-eight, or twenty-three per cent.

At one practice group meeting (where each solicitor would update the group on their current activities), a colleague reporting on a case gave a lengthy physical description of his female client before relaying the relevant details of the case. I looked around the table to read people's faces. The female partner caught my eye and winked. We had rarely spoken previously but this gesture let me know that she also believed the solicitor was out of line. Small clues like this are important to reassure young women that the reconnaissance party has gone ahead and chartered the possible obstacles, in order that we might successfully avoid them.

Since then I have changed jobs. Now I have the opportunity to be part of an organisation that just happens to be made up only of female lawyers. The receptionist is a male law student who makes the tea and coffee happily. Initially, the notion of a pocket of sororial solidarity in the sea of the legal fraternity seemed like a breath of fresh air. But in a short time, it became apparent that sisterhood alone is no binding factor. Not everyone you meet can offer an apprenticeship. I realise that there is no automatic connection between women by virtue of sex alone. Even if all of the staff (including men) regard themselves as feminists, this does not mean that we will necessarily agree to all (or any) matters of methodology. The organisation, for example, had many views on how disputes should be resolved, how performance should be measured and on organisational structure.

I am fortunate to have the mentorship of a colleague in this organisation. She was the first person in a workplace who told me I was smart, that I had good ideas, that my work was of a high standard. It was not only a compliment but an incredible relief, and I began working more autonomously and more productively. She used me as a sounding board for ideas about alternative approaches to legal problems and sought my opinions about the direction of the organisation. The more my opinion was respected, the more I endeavoured to develop ideas that could contribute to the workplace. I studied her analysis of issues, responded to her challenges and learned to defend my stances when they differed from hers. It has become the most valuable and the most satisfying working relationship I have had.

There are times when the challenges of my work threaten to overwhelm me. Sometimes my reaction is to rush to my mentor and ask for "the answer", knowing that it will come easily to her but would take me considerable time to discover. This is nearly always a mistake. She often reminds me that her role is not simply to pass me the key to the door but only to give me clues as to where I might find it. The mentor role is not as benevolent as a fairy godmother. Quite the contrary. The challenges she poses can be frustrating: the distinction between mentor and tormentor can feel like a fine one at times.

Knowing the value of mentorships, I now have the opportunity to develop them with juniors. As a female lawyer, I see this as my responsibility. I must be assertive and speak out about matters which affect me personally, and address inequalities where I see them, offering support and leadership to other women. Without young women harnessing the experiences of others, success in the workplace becomes a matter of ineffective guesswork, especially for those who have not determined how to translate the lessons learned from our teenage role models. As long as systemic discrimination continues to construct the legal workplace as male, and until women reach the senior ranks in numbers equal to men, mentoring offers one way of keeping female contenders on track.

While it would be reassuring to think that there might be someone looking out for you throughout your career, especially during the challenges of the early days, we should not expect to be watched over by guardian angels forever. Furthermore it is possible to outgrow the person or the workplace. When this happens, we fly the coop and thank our benefactor and take up the mantle. A mentor is less like a co-pilot and more like a ground control tower: once you have been directed to the right runway and forewarned about the nature of air traffic, the take off is up to you.

Finding My Feminism[*]

Kate Lundy

I t is difficult for me to recall the shy teenager who stripped asbestos and demolished buildings for a living. I began my career as a labourer on a building site after answering an advertisement in the local paper. With only relatively brief work experience behind the counter at the local McDonalds, I decided that the construction industry held far greater appeal.

In retrospect, this was quite a brave move for a sixteen-year-old girl. Securing the labouring job was a great confidence booster, despite the fib about my age to get

---

[*] This chapter originated as a speech given at the Queen's Trust Forum for Young Australians, in Melbourne, 11 July, 1997.

through the front door. The work was uncomfortable and required long periods in extreme temperatures while wearing respirators and protective clothing. The decontamination procedures associated with asbestos removal required six showers per day. The other workers on site were terrific and made me feel welcome. We were all different and I learned quickly to respect these differences.

Working on a building site taught me a great deal about life. More, I believe, than any other job could have, at that time. Those years shaped me, and instilled in me a real understanding of what it is like to be at the bottom of the pile. Then, I didn't think that there would be much more for me beyond the site. I had a chip on my shoulder and I was considered quite an angry young woman.

Being a member of the construction industry also compared favourably to being stereotyped as a "teenage no-hoper". I genuinely took pride in sweeping the floor just right, and scouring the asbestos off structural steel with my trusty barbecue scraper and blue plastic brush.

My interest in unions arose from very practical and personal concerns about occupational health and safety. There came a time when I started to weigh my future health against the week's wage packet, and I realised that perhaps there was some substance to the fears about inhaling the flaky white stuff that we worked with every day. Despite the respirators and protective clothing, there were real risks associated with carcinogenic fibres. For me, the union's assertion that "every worker has the right to a safe and healthy workplace" was enough to spark an interest that has since become a lifelong commitment.

When I became the site union delegate, the Building Workers Industrial Union (BWIU) became my entry into the political world. I found my work as a delegate difficult, awkward and embarrassing. I couldn't address my work-mates without blushing profusely.

This experience and my efforts as delegate soon led to an offer of temporary work as an organiser with the ACT Branch of the BWIU. I remember being immensely proud and flattered when offered this job, and I was brave enough to say yes. My strength in this role came from two years of practical experience in the industry. The union's political dimension brought me into contact with many progressive individuals and organisations. I was on a vertical learning curve during those first few years with the union.

As an organiser in the union, one of the most difficult experiences was confronting a new site with 400 building workers I'd never met before. I didn't know whether they were hostile to the union, and I didn't know how they'd take a girl telling them what to do. In this situation, I would drive around the block three times, each time repeating "If I can do this, I can do anything". I still say if you can handle 400 building workers who have spent their lunchtime at the pub, then you can handle any-thing. In subsequent years, that experience really helped me.

About this time I was asked to stand in the union elections. I subsequently became the first woman elected to the BWIU executive. I always received great support from my male colleagues, but at this point I still did not consciously link the opportunities presented to me with the struggle for equal rights for women.

When I was eighteen, I joined the Australian Labor Party (ALP) because it seemed like a party that could effectively represent me, as a young working woman. At that time, I hadn't mastered words like "social justice", and I didn't know about "discrimination" or "feminism". As a result, my first couple of years in the ALP were an awakening, in the true sense. I learned the words which went with my thoughts and feelings about what was fair and right.

During these times, I remember being impressed by the strong women who had their say at ALP branch meetings, and in some cases ran the show! The ALP seemed to satisfy everything I was looking for in political representation, and there were plenty of other women already there reinforcing this perception.

At the outset of my career with the union I knew little about feminism and what it meant. I was never sure what to say when in the company of women who I knew were feminists. My confidence would nose-dive and I was sure that my ignorance would undermine the political credibility that I was working so hard to build. As a result, I didn't ask questions.

I distinctly remember the conversation that gave me my first insight into feminism. The conversation was sparked by a flippant comment I made about never having perceived a problem getting a job in the construction industry. It took me a few days to get over the response from my female colleague. Gone was my naive recollection about how I had secured my "first real job". In its place was a sobering dose of reality. Many questions later, the story unfolded: I had been employed because the union insisted that half the company's new intake be women. I was one of few who had applied.

So why had the union insisted on my employment? A few months earlier, in March 1984, the federal parliament had passed the *Sex Discrimination Act* and the unions were using their industrial muscle to ensure that its principles were exercised promptly in the well-organised sectors of the construction industry. So much for my phenomenal interviewing skills and instinctive common sense!

Initially I was angry about these revelations. I interpreted it as a failing on my part; as though it wasn't my achievement at all. I had been brought up to believe in gender equality, but suddenly, this assumption was shattered. I realised that women face significant barriers. But I was cautious not to dismiss equality outright. I knew it had to be true because it made sense of so many contradictions I had experienced. Besides, the Act had also served to recruit me to the cause!

This relatively brief conversation ended up having a profound impact on my world view. It established new ideals and added another layer to my political understanding. It forced me to analyse the situation facing women more closely, and feminists ceased to be such a mystery. Indeed, my experience was a positive, practical vindication of the work of thousands of women spanning generations and I marvelled at their persistence and motivation. For me, the powerful ideological connection between the Women's Movement and the left-wing of the labour movement reinforced the relevance of feminism.

Almost as suddenly as I had chanced upon it, there was no more equivocation in my feminism. I wanted to be part of the Movement and I felt a powerful responsibility to contribute to the ongoing campaign for equity. I began taking a serious interest in the position of women in the workplace. I also gained my first insight into the role of the labour movement in improving women's status in society.

I often wonder why I didn't see the structural barriers and the active discrimination during my schooling and in my early years of work experience. Using rudimentary logic, I figured that if I had made assumptions about equality throughout school, then boys must have as well. As I didn't complete Year 11 – let alone go to university – I presumed that this must be where young women and men were introduced to feminism. However, discussions with young people suggest that this is not always the case.

Maybe then the workplace is responsible for introducing young people to the structural discrimination against women. Despite the sexist stereotype of the building site worker, the construction industry contains a remarkable mix of attitudes shaped by generation, ethnicity and experience. Nevertheless, the Sexual Discrimination Act played a critical role in raising awareness and legislating against previously unacceptable forms of behaviour. Just having women on site was the most powerful circuit breaker to entrenched sexist behaviour.

Some people accept feminism's many claims without question; others acknowledge sexism and deal with it as best they can. Still others are motivated to become active campaigners, including through unions or human resources management structures. In the BWIU, the nature of my work was entirely conducive to joining campaigns and identifying myself as a feminist. I started to think about reaching other young women.

My interpretation of feminism is very personal, and its development has contributed significantly to my sense of self. My life experience is one of manual work, motherhood and politics. I never anticipated a representative role in the Australian Parliament.

I am not a lawyer, academic or businesswoman. My formal qualifications consist of a Year 10 Certificate, scaffolder's licence and hoist driver's ticket. I have managed to balance family and work, and this balance is my measure of personal achievement.

I am confident that my life experience has relevance in the context of my current work. However, this wasn't always the case. When I first considered standing for the Senate, I went through an internal process of dispelling self-doubt. How important is an academic degree? Is intellectual credibility a prerequisite for a parliamentary career? Surely it must be. I asked myself what the hell I was doing, contemplating election to federal parliament.

Over a period of time, the answers came. I realised that my experiences and political opinions are as valid as anyone's. Diversity strengthens Australian society and if our parliaments are to be truly representative, this diversity must be reflected there. I came to the conclusion that if a semi-educated labourer with two young children can be elected, then this was a positive reflection of our democratic system.

In my view, a number of personal credentials are important for anyone contemplating a career in politics. A strong sense of social responsibility is the most important prerequisite, along with a genuine commitment to advancing society. Commitment to governance in the interest of the public is the ultimate test of social responsibility. To me, this requires acknowledgment of the important role played by the public sector in our society. Failure to do this can only lead to social imbalance.

There are some politicians who have nothing to offer but division and diversion, preferring to place rampant ideology before social responsibility. In combination, these factors can lead to a further breakdown in the people's confidence in our democratic structures. In a disturbing trend, this decline in confidence is being exploited by political opportunists. Detailed analysis of the "values" of different sections of the community make it possible for parties to target these voters with emotive messages. Most Australians are not politically active and this general apathy in turn makes voters vulnerable to issues that trigger principles and prejudices. This tactical approach to securing votes is known as "wedge politics".

Australia today is certainly different from what it was, even as recently as a few years ago. For many of us, that difference is not a cause for celebration. Social justice is not a feature of the current government's agenda. But new ideas, different perspectives and diversity of experiences are critical ingredients to any political organisation – particularly a party in opposition. Communicating these ideas represents a massive challenge. As a politician, a big part of my role is conveying the ALP's ideas, in the hope that like-minded people will identify with them and stimulate the interest and support of others.

People with an interest in political activity face many barriers. First, extensive demands on our time mean that very few people are able to devote themselves to a new or ongoing cause. As a result, personal priorities determine our political involvement. I know this from when I was working on building sites. There, I would prioritise union responsibilities against work, social activities and sleep – all life's necessities, and that was before I had children!

It is not surprising that the most politically active people are those whose lives (and livelihoods) are influenced directly by political decisions. My experience bears this out. As a labourer, my health was protected by occupational health and safety laws. The inadequacy of these laws was originally the issue that raised my political consciousness. It wasn't workers' rights or global peace. These "big picture" issues have become fragmented and young Australians are increasingly politicised in single-issue or narrowly defined campaigns, driving social justice and similar philosophies down the list of political priorities.

Yet I believe that social justice remains the most important philosophical issue facing Australian society today. Social justice emerges from our sense of community, which both entitles everyone to individual freedoms, but also assigns social responsibilities. It is our role as members of a community to look after other people as best we are able. We should reach out with a helping hand to those in need. Life is not a Darwinian model of survival of the fittest. All members of our community must be protected by a safety net that prevents destitution and despair. Being part of a community means recognising that those who do not succeed are not victims, but people in need of assistance from government. A caring, harmonious society that addresses the needs of the elderly, young, disabled, unemployed and disenfranchised is more important than having a healthy bottom line.

At times, I have questioned my own ability to alter the structures and attitudes of our society that restrict progress. But time and time again, I have been amazed at the difference one person can make and this has served me well as inspiration.

My path was to become involved with a political party that encouraged me to participate. Being active in the labour movement both industrially and politically has made me hopeful for the future. I have changed from a despairing teenager into a person who feels that a positive contribution to society is both possible and achievable.

I know that I am perceived as a leader by some, but that label is just one of the many that I am proud of. I am also, amongst other things, a mother, a daughter, a unionist, an adviser, a friend, a rower and a Senator. Recognising the political value of my experiences as a woman has shaped my contributions. Our contributions to society are not narrow; they are not only a vocation or career. Instead, we contribute as whole people.

To be politically active, in whatever capacity, is to be empowered. In pursuit of our own ideals we seek to inspire others to affect change. The challenge is huge for both parties and individuals. How can we turn apathy into interest? Interest into understanding? And understanding into opinion and activism? Part of the answer to these questions can be found in the systems and structures that constitute our democracy. But the answer also depends on our ability to communicate effectively, and on the credibility of politicians.

I am a beneficiary of feminism's campaign for gender equality. Along with bravery and a strong sense of social justice, this has made it possible for me to participate in Australian politics as a Senator. I still pinch myself occasionally and reflect on the vehemence of my cynicism in earlier years – what wasted energy! Optimism fuels hope and hope predicates progressive change. And it is far easier to be optimistic about the future if you are part of the process that shapes it. I am proud to be there.

Bodies

& Battlefields

Drawing the Frontline: Love, Sex and Revenge

Jo Dyer

We called ourselves WARS. Women Attack Rampant Sexism. We got very angry if media organisations called us Women *Against* Rampant Sexism. We were attacking – actively fighting, not against, passively opposing. Our press release began, "Forget Hewson's Fightback, it's time for women to fight back!".[1] We may not have been poets but we were certainly angry. We formed – all two of us – an urban vigilante pseudo–terrorist organisation that roamed the streets late at night throwing bricks and warnings through

---

1 "Fightback!" was the Liberal Party campaign slogan, for Australia's 1993 federal election.

the windows of newsagents who refused to remove demeaning pictures of naked women from their banner displays. You know the pictures – naked breasts, prostrate women, dog collars, leashes and chains, all on the front cover of a magazine. We were delighted when the media thought we were a whole network of fervent activist zealots. We had our photos taken for a page three story wearing balaclavas. The photographer was a pacifist and could barely disguise his distaste for us. We laughed snidely, just as we laughed when the newsagent cut his hand cleaning up the broken glass. Our laughter was captured on national television, despite the purdah-style veil the TV interviewer had persuaded us to don.

We embraced notoriety and thought little of credibility. Our anger was our shield from criticism.

This was around the time when the most fashionable dinner parties debated whether all penetration was rape. None of us had been raped but we'd all been penetrated, so felt infinitely if not exclusively qualified to comment. We didn't denigrate penetration *in toto*, as we tended to engage in it quite a bit, and while those synonymising rape and penetration argued consent was impossible in a patriarchal world, we didn't think ourselves brainwashed. Like car accidents, false consciousness always happens to other people – have you noticed? We hedged our bets and said while we may not espouse the theory ourselves, there was nonetheless, a persuasive argument to support the idea that penetrative sex is nothing more than rape. Certainly, the chief proponents of this theory, Andrea Dworkin and Catharine MacKinnon, were great thinkers and defenders of women in a violent and hostile society (as indeed were we).

Our cleverness and controversy delighted us. We infuriated our male associates by asserting our subordination in superior tones, and flaunted our feminist credentials with demonstrations of emotional self-sufficiency. Emotional autonomy was really the key to it – none of that dependence or vulnerability for us. We were onto the myth of romantic love from an early age, and avoided any threats to our independence by incredulous exposure of ludicrous plots to seduce us with words of love. Such declarations were either poor facades to cover the onset of relationships of calculated exploitation, or were setting us up for humiliating and public rejection in front of our hitherto admiring peers. Anything less than complete independence was a clear indication of weakness, completely inexcusable and a recipe for disaster. This we knew, and we weren't afraid to enlighten everyone else – in loud and declamatory tones.

It was a cunning ploy, really. The use of political ideology as a means for escaping intimacy. Who wouldn't be defensive when charged with the responsibility of defending an entire gender from persistent and pernicious attack? And we felt it difficult, even hypocritical, to assert one's feminist credentials, to sneer by day that men are negative and manipulative, when by night you lick the sweat from their brow with your tongue. Is it still a frontline if you're fucking, and not fighting? Can it be a frontline if you're fucking? What about if you make it the frontline *because* you're fucking?

Statistics will show I was always up for the fight.

Alcohol had a lot to do with it. Alcohol and restlessness set my anger on roam. We've all had those evenings when (cheap) wine in vast quantities is desperately consumed to release the wit and raconteur imprisoned deep within. Night and words slip past and out, and at the end of it all the bottle you clutch holds less (red) wine than your (white) shirt, and your brain seems equally empty. You've been chatting to a bloke with an eloquence as surprising as liquid, and the time soon comes to lurch away in an unspoken pact that will see you grappling with each other – in a car or a bed or maybe just around the corner – in the none too distant future.

It was all a bit of a game – a new and adult party game – an amusing strategy of hit and run.

See darling, it was all planned. A sentence or two, a sideways glance – can you do a smouldering invitation in a drunken hot stare? Loud laughter – the crowd's with me – and before you knew it, the joys of my thin single bed. With each conquest, a small blow for feminism, a proud demonstration of women's transient needs, of the inherent expendability of men in the brave new world of female autonomy. Promiscuity as political activism – I had found my niche. It was a type of reverse psychology I brought to bear. Appalled by the saturation sexualising of women in our society, I went on a one woman campaign to even the score. No matter how smart you were (or how smart you thought you were) I made sure you knew it wasn't your fine intellect that got you into bed. No matter how intelligent, how funny, how charming, once the deed was done, on your bike!

For all those men who have seduced women with their laughter and their looks, who have been the substance of their dreams and the reason for their hope; for the men who have done the gazing and the ones who made the move, for the ones who won't hear "no" when it's shouted, or won't say yes again, for the men who never rang, and the ones who never stopped – I was on a sweeping, searing trajectory of revenge.

Anxiety, uncertainty, displacement, fear – these were men's gift to women, rather than humanity's blessed curse. And it was my job to turn the tables.

Clearly, sexual gratification didn't feature highly. It was all about power. There was a bit of obligatory moaning, sure, and if the energy was up, a spot of writhing. But the pursuit of physical enjoyment was not a factor on nights such as these, and sensation ran a poor second to intensive mental monitoring. How long have we been going? Is he having fun, or just going through the motions? Should I have come yet? Have I come yet? If I haven't, does he know? If I pretend to, will he stop? Awaiting or expecting waves of pleasure were dangerous distractions from the primary goal of staying conscious and/or planning his eviction. Indeed, to be swept away by passion ceded the point and the power. Own goal. Orgasm as embarrassment. Defeat by enjoyment.

The only problem with my tenacious campaign was that despite the smug political satisfaction it afforded me, it didn't make for great sex. As a military strategy, it worked very well: I always had the element of surprise on my side. My manoeuvres were so successful that the opponent would often never know he was anything more than a casual partner.

As a seasoned and decorated fighter on the battlefield, I believed I would always be prepared. I was vigilant, after all. Suspicious. On guard. Somebody had to be. But I was not prepared for someone coming along who seemed to be in love with me, and appeared to be a trustworthy type (the worst ones?). And rather than the ultimate weapon in the gender war, he thought sex was a sacred site of intimacy through which you can communicate and demonstrate the depth of your feeling for each other (does he expect me to marry him, bear his children, be his domestic slave?) And the more vulnerable you are, apparently, the better the sex. Strip away the layers.

I was supposed to throw down my weapons, cease my patrol, and open myself up to joy. And I actually wanted to (may god – in all her mercy – please forgive me). Unfortunately, I was as equipped to do this as to surf a river of Mercury.

It's a tricky one. Sex as war slightly undermines sex as enjoyable pastime, and it stymies the fracturingly intimate moments love affairs are ostensibly all about. When you think about it, the very characteristics of being in love are anathema to the idea of being a feminist. If you're in love, you get used to the idea of throwing yourself into the tumult of passion, of riding the waves of joy and emotion. Your lover comes first, first in everything. At the very least, you jealously guard his needs and his desires in an omniscient, omnipresent kind of way. Sacrifice all for your love. Lay down your life for your love. (Allow yourself to be completely exploited by your lover in a relationship which is inherently unequal? By a *man*?)

Never mind the specifics, we're talking big picture. And the big picture said I needed to look out first and foremost for me and my needs. My needs and desires are first priority and indeed, second, third and only priority. Otherwise watch the ground give way beneath your feet as you fall straight into the patriarchal trap (well disguised underfoot by the leaves, love and shit), and before you know it, it's the male's needs at the expense of your own. And then the kiddies' needs and did you have your own? Think about complaining, and you're on your own. I'd read all about it, and it was smart strategy. Be in love, be monogamous, be a wife, be a mother, be domesticated and then exploited in, and by that economic model sometimes known as the (patriarchal) family.

Where did it all come from, this mistrust and suspicion? Some of it was my own peculiar take on my less than peculiar circumstances growing up. Isn't it always? We're all so busy being desperately unique, it's almost demoralising to observe how conventionally we can respond to impossibly conventional situations.

I lived in a house full of girls, all growing up unwittingly afraid of the explosive temper of our unengaging, absent father. He never hit us, but he had a great range of violent shouting that covered us in spittle as we cowered, unconvincingly defiant. He upped and left in the middle of my final year exams – I boasted about it to my classmates, demonstrating how cool I could be. Emotions, who needs 'em, who's got 'em? His departure came as a shock to us mainly because we didn't know he had it in him. All too aware of his unattractive idiosyncrasies, we were oblivious to his late nights and transparent stories. He didn't go with any grace, either. It was a lengthy process – tacky and tawdry – punctuated with tears. I became an expert at solemn recitations of his sins, at knowing revelations of his bastardry. I wisely, then impatiently, counselled my mother on the benefits of a clean clear break, of the sense in making and keeping firm resolutions about moving forward, not looking back. My mother's refusal to accept easily – if not cheerfully – the great chasm in her life, where once she'd had a husband, enraged me. Her bids to change his mind with entreaties and tantrums disgusted me. What terrible displays – demeaning, I thought haughtily, especially for a feminist. What of the creed of fish and bicycles – men were meant to be anachronistic, dispensable and ridiculous. Wasn't feminism about female independence? So why was my mother crying deep into the night, why were great goblets of gin her mandatory nightcaps, and how could I ensure that never happened to me?

It's easy to take a blast of hot rage spawned by abandonment and betrayal, and channel it through into shock and resolve, before packing it down into a small stone of bitterness. Like geology. Layered and layered. It's diffuse. All men, not father. Anger, not pain. It's ideology, not emotion. A just war.

A war fought on behalf of the murdered women. When police find the bodies and question estranged or crazy spouses. A war to even the score with the serial killers – when brutal violent men play out their fantasies across the bodies of young dead women. We learn about their victims – often familiar types. In Perth last year, it was a girl I could have known. Private school, then to law school, pleased to be there, life mapped out. Studied hard, did well, and dreamt one day of leading her parents' lives. Corporate law firm, expensive suits, big cases, low heels, nice income. Litigation by day and stark pubs with iron railings in the inner city at night. And then a brutal, violent moment with a brutal, violent man, and she's panicking, and she's terrified, and she's about to die. Her worst nightmares are coming true in slow motion – they do for some people. Not like false consciousness. This could happen to you. And you try not to generalise, and you love your male friends dearly, but someone loved that man too, and he's just raped and murdered a girl like me.

In Afghanistan, women aren't allowed out the front door. The Taliban keeps them safely hidden from the world, under cloth. A gender disappears, and the world is relieved at the end of a war. In India and China, female foetuses are identified through the wonders of modern technology, and greeted by a scalpel to make way for the boys. Death by patriarchy. A generation without little girls. Growing into a generation without women. It's easy to nurture an anger, rage bubbling like nausea.

Even the "enlightened" West can raise my ire. The distribution of power is far from equal – we've only got two genders, where's the problem? Yet the fight for equality attracts such scorn from those who think the war is over. The pendulum has swung too far; we're humourless and grasping, we deserve everything we get. I feel my stone of bitterness burn with my eyes. I close over and down with suspicion and dismay. A great source of the inequality in Western society is indisputably the home, particularly for women with childcare responsibilities. Their great joy and curse is their children. The single biggest factor affecting the amount of time women devote to domestic labour is the presence of children – far more decisive than working outside the home. So much time and energy is devoted to rearing children, there's precious little left to spend chasing a career. Perhaps a part-time job – to get out of the house. But as more jobs become casual, and less well paid, and childcare becomes more expensive, less affordable, it's difficult to see a radical change in the current trends pushing women out of the work-force and back into homes and positions of economic dependency. Wives love their husbands, but in a society where nearly fifty per cent of marriages end in divorce, and eighty per cent of households in poverty are headed by single mothers, it's hard to call it good planning to let him provide for you. That the home is the greatest site of violence for women, and male family members the most common perpetrators of this violence, only serves to harden the heavy sharp stone.

Recent years have seen the splintering of the sisterhood too, as more privileged women begin to buy the domestic labour of their working-class sisters to escape its drudgery themselves. While some may believe it is enough to stride around capably with mobile and filofax in soft leather briefcase, I for one, am a firm supporter of feminism requiring one to help someone other than oneself. An ability to pick a good pinstripe and a large pay-cheque doth not an overwhelming contribution to feminism make! The right-on enthusiasm of riot grrls and cyber chicks surfing with attitude is also unlikely to achieve real and lasting material change down here in our all too material world. Chat rooms populated by like-minded folk of indeterminate gender typing with one hand won't be the engine rooms of change.

Paranoid disdain of men and their strange, large, frightening power, enmeshed with fear and anxieties surrounding vulnerability, can somehow leave one feeling so at risk. Raise your swords, call the battle-cry, and prepare for the most Pyrrhic of all victories. If you're hurtling along in your chariot of war, tricky gear changes in motion are notoriously tough, and they're not the manoeuvres in which we're practised. Untangling powerful and righteous anger at society's injustices from the confused chaos of personal relationships is crucial if you want to have a good relationship with one of these beasts, let alone a partnership. Calm down, take a deep breath, cleave through your brain's cotton wool, open your head and your heart, and together talk through the white fuzz of confusion.

Naked Feminism

Louisa Smith

My naked body melts into the white sheets. Drooping, bulging, curving, falling, dimpling, rippling. Like an Joan Semmel painting, the picture begins with the neck and shoulders, breasts, rounded tummy, fleshy hips, pubic hair, touching thighs and little feet. People often tell me I have a figure like an hour glass. "Where's the sand?" I ask. They never reply, so I tell them there is no sand. This is my body, it is warm, it is mine.

I have a journal. It has a black cover and white pages. Each page is a map to my mind; each drawing a friend of my subconscious, each realisation a child of my brain. As I re-read, I am cast back through periods of enlightenment. I realise that this black book is not just filled with words but the story of a search. It is my means of mapping my self. The pages walk, run, leap and stumble through struggles and conflicts. The little book becomes a means of catharsis, untangling and reorganising my confusion, leaving a written portrait, an attempt at photographing my mind. I have discovered a great deal about myself through my journal. But it seems impossible to fully understand who I am, until I understand who we are. What is woman? What does this body I look at, and that I live in, mean? I must search beyond myself to answer these questions.

I begin with my friends. In a climactic moment of conversation, my friends and I discovered a desire to share our ideas about being female, and we decided we'd begin with each other. We bought another book with a black cover to serve as our collective journal; it became a medium of shared written contemplation. And we wrote. As my friends lay naked on the pages, we discovered something new about ourselves and each other. While we took words from Shakespeare and de Beauvoir, it was the simple words of my friends which had most meaning. Pages emanated dreams, fantasy and colour. As with my journal, this book showed that each of my friends was on a search. There is something comforting in knowing that others face similar questions and quandaries.

Momentarily, I was content to limit myself to this small movement of women. But these women were my friends, my friends who shared my interests and had grown up in similar circumstances. It follows that we would have similar feelings and ambitions. What about other women? What about women from the past? I questioned what "thing" made us women.

As women, we may be unified by our bodies: breasts, vaginas, wombs. To me the female body is magic. It is a sacred vessel, and if all is well, it can grow and sustain life within it. Previously, the female "monopoly" over procreation meant that society determined the primary female function as that of child-bearer. Thus body has dictated destiny. Even eighteen years ago, at my birth, my body earned me pink dresses and dolls. Fortunately, my brother was given trucks and we traded toys. As a child, I was unaware that we were disobeying the expectations of our genders, but looking back, I am grateful to my parents for respecting our innocent exchange.

Many women have not been so fortunate; their female bodies imposing limitations upon their actions, their lives. The body is often seen as the enemy and the prohibiter of freedoms enjoyed by men. Adam and Eve shamefully covered their bodies with Eden's leaves; this shame is echoed by the pretty, discreet tampon box with a euphemistic name hidden in the bottom of my bag, as if to disguise a "curse". Recently, I arrived at a party wearing a transparent top which exposed parts of my breasts; I was ordered by a male friend to put a jacket on because I "looked like a slut". Like Eve, I was expected to cover my female "bits" and keep them for private acts of passion. Through this denial of our bodies, we hide something which unifies us; as if it is shameful to have a female body.

Western society promotes feelings of shame about the female body. Just as idealistic representations of the male body are prevalent in Greek art, today's idealised female body assumes a form which is unrealistic for most of the population. Shopping last week, I was reminded of the contemporary ideal: revealing bones, small breasts, indistinguishable hips and, preferably, blackened eyes. Shop windows glow with cartoonish female forms. I recall the body of Michelangelo's *David*. Whereas no man was ever expected to attain the religious and bodily perfection of David, the models in department store windows wear clothes made for apparently mortal women. Today's female shape is small and curve-less. I find myself conscious of my hips and bottom and this self consciousness is exacerbated by shopping expeditions. As I go from shop to shop trying to find a funky, youthful pair of pants, I become increasingly resentful of my body which does not flatter the fashionable skimpy jeans I dreamed of, and which looked so good in the window. I find myself tramping back to a store where size twelve means twelve. During the bus ride home, nursing the neatly made, tailored, classic pants, I realise that I am not only tired and deflated but also sad. I am sad because the body I love is not loved by society. Yet my body is not unhealthy; it just doesn't match an ideal because its female "bits" are too big – my breasts and my hips swell and protrude. Again, I feel embarrassed by what is distinctly female about my body.

When I was thirteen, I thought sex would be like sport. You need to know the rules, wear protection, have a high level of fitness, develop skills and practise. When you become involved in the game, you realise you're not playing with a racquet or a stick; your weapon is your body. Lying skin to skin, you become aware that no referee will blow the whistle for foul play. When the clothes come off and the ball is in play, only you can throw up your hands for a penalty. As a naive, probably hormone-driven young woman, I recently found myself stuck between my white sheets and a strong, heavy man. I'd obviously missed this part of the rule book, because when I expressed my hesitations he did not attempt to move off me. Instead, he looked me in the eyes, becoming heavier and heavier. I could not move. He did not move. Out of my mouth came "I can't, I've got my period". I still wonder why I said it. I knew that the prospect of a yucky red mess would deter an inexperienced boy like him. However, it frightens me that my automatic reaction was to use a bodily function rather than a simple rejection to halt everything. Perhaps I was fighting his bodily strength with my bodily fluids. I didn't have my period and he knew it, but he rolled off me all the same. It scared him that my body was more than just warm breasts in a heated moment. To him, this was more than sport, it was ritual. Interrupted ritual.

Talking to one of my male friends, I asked him for his views about sex. Quite triumphantly, he defined it as "a commodity to be purchased as often as possible". Without wishing to excuse this attitude, for him sexual pleasure was always a matter of a hand and a minute. Another friend attempted to convince me that the mere sight of a woman can stimulate an erection and that masturbation was a daily necessity to relieve sexual tension. For me, sex means something very different. My sexual pleasure is internal, intimate and intensely personal; it is almost impossible to align it with a game of hockey – except perhaps for the sweat.

When I am with a group of women, I feel unity and a sense of understanding. I feel a unity because we share a body, a body which shares a history of being discarded, restricted and violated. And so between women there is an empathy and understanding concerning our experiences, and how these will be affected by our bodies. There is also a unity which stems from women's experiences of their bodies; be it menstruation, sex, sexuality or childbirth. I remember when, after a few too many beers, two of my female friends gave me a graphic sex education lesson, with hands, tongues and teeth manipulating the air. It was an unforgettable demonstration of shared female knowledge.

When I sit with a group of friends, I am surrounded by intelligent and active women, all wanting something different from life. Some want success, others seek leisure; some are Christian or pagan and others call themselves nothing, in case they change their minds; some want money and others don't. Similarly, on many evenings I have sat sipping tea with my mother's friends: teachers, lawyers, painters, doctors and mothers. Despite their differences these women are united as they are women who wish to be themselves. They act as they choose, and for this reason, I call us all feminists.

I have often found myself shying away from the word feminism, in fear of being labelled lesbian, aggressive or outdated. Only yesterday, I explained some of my thoughts in this chapter to a friend. Another at the table politely asked me if I was a lesbian. He then apologised adding that as a short-haired feminist I should expect such inquiries.

As I search for a common female identity and a sense of unity among women, I find myself echoing the experiences of many women, whose paths forged the foundation of feminism.

So I say proudly that I am a feminist. I am a feminist because I want my female body to complement what I do. I see my female body as a privilege which allows me the choice of bearing a child. And I am a feminist because I love being a woman; especially a woman who has a voice.

Weighing in as a Feminist

Debra Shulkes

Sitting in your house then, did you notice
how I didn't have any words yet to shout aloud?
My mouth hung open as a lidless bottle
Letting my insides go flat as dead lemonade . . .

From my diary, 1993.

I am going to begin with a confession that seems to me to be startling less for its content than for the sheer number of similar stories that I have heard related among so many of my successful women friends. Prevalent as it is, it always surfaces abruptly, bobbing awkwardly as a lone yellow floatie in the public pool of our conversations. Experience suggests that I should save my confessions for the talk show circuit. I should squeeze these narratives of embarrassment and shame into unsigned, serial letters to a magazine doctor. Yet I find myself wanting to lay my huddle of confessional words down at the beginning. I am writing in the hope that I can shift those experiences I once assumed to be squalid and strictly personal into the register of the political and public. But even now with my hands perched on the keyboard, I catch myself feeling frightened: it seems I need to pause, to walk around the room, I need to reconsider the outcomes before I tell you that I was anorexic when I was seventeen.

I have noticed that whenever I talk about this period of my life, I explain it like one of those four-week, neatly resolved plot lines on an American high school drama series. I say that it was brief and unexpected, a teenage hiccough. My guess is that it is the shocking shadows that gather around the word anorexia that cause me to hurry my speech: the word unnerves me, whichever font I meet it in. I run away from both the arrogant, bold print of *The Diagnostic and Statistical Manual of Psychiatric Disorders*,[1] and the fluorescent blue type of magazines revealing "devastating secrets" and "the scariest photos ever". The truth is that neither of these accounts – neither the psychiatric label nor the anorexic-outing magazine – with their shared interests in portraying anorexia as a freakish individual pathology, comes close to tapping into my seventeen-year-old mentality. Neither is awake to the terrifying equation of thinness with success and opportunity that my peers and I, the freed-up young women who finished school in the early 1990s, inherited. Similarly, neither notices the routine way in which we, the inhabitants of a post-feminist era, were taught that our worth could be read off the curvature of our stomachs.

---

1   *The Diagnostic and Statistical Manual of Psychiatric Disorders* (*DSM–IV*) (1994). A tool used by psychiatrists to diagnose disorders. A doctor, psychiatrist or therapist tallies symptoms and a patient's disorder, condition or mental illness is identified and diagnosed.

It may seem strange that the generation of women hyped as the beneficiaries of feminism should have been so ruled by a tyranny of slimness. But my experience tells me that this was the case. And whatever the media said about the shattering of glass ceilings and the availability of DIY success, we still felt trapped by the size of our bodies. My own head spun with contradictions: I was highly suspicious of the construction of malnutrition as a female ideal and yet, whenever I reflected, I found myself in the state of feeling too fat. I was keen to travel and explore the world, but also intent on shrinking the space I occupied, on trying quite literally to go away. Like the laws of physics, dieting facts had a stunning reality. They described the immutable truth of my position in the world, and spoke with the plummy severity of my British primary school teacher: "You need to eat less to weigh less. Sugar is a no-no. Decline a second slice." Thus, even as I tried to dodge the pressure to look skeletal in lycra, when I sat outside the library, lost in the pastel fog of *Cosmopolitan*, the fleshy excess of my body was conspicuous. I felt I was a product with assets and deficits, and my body was a gross surplus (in every sense). And I sensed the herculean effort it would take to unglue my feet from this old, ingrained position.

Like a 1920s flapper sucking in and binding flesh in order to attain that carefree, boyish style, I had long understood skinniness to be a critical (but unspoken) part of the new liberal package of opportunities, freedom and daring for women. A basic tenet of my education was that the world is a level playing field, yielding opportunities for hardworking individuals. It was articulated, for instance, in an article I clipped by a pre-*Beauty Myth* Naomi Wolf:

> *My friends and I are the first women in history who were*
> *brought up to take access into any institution as a given: if*
> *we were good enough, we were told, it would be ours – and*
> *astonishingly, up through the rarefied arena of a university*
> *like Yale, it is* (cited in Chernin: 1981, p. 29).

Perhaps the reason I so clearly remember reading and clipping the Wolf piece is that it invoked the relentless challenge to be "good enough" – a challenge I had been familiar with for a very long time. When I was anorexic, this challenge tormented me more than anything, maybe because it was around that time that I realised "good" was always going to resist a fixed definition. You could not equate it with an exact height-weight ratio or a school certificate or a winner's pure aluminium teaspoon. Rather, good was an amorphous, unspecific quality, meaning in my mind, diligent, self-determined, successful and/or thin. The rewards of being good alone seemed clear: I reeled them off like the desired qualities in a personals advertisement: social ease, money, joy in life (I might have added a sense of humour, no tattoos, please).

As long as I strived to be good, I was staking everything on amassing a list of socially recognisable achievements some time in the future. There was a constant sing-song deferral of happiness, of trembling conditionals in my head: "If only I can win this prize/ receive this mark/ write one short story this year/ lose enough weight/ then things will be all right, I'll cope." Even so, I found that every time I stopped struggling, stopped huff-puffing up the ladder with no last rung in sight, I was left standing terrified or staring at my goose bumps. I looked at those tiny humps and the irately raised hairs on my arms as though my body belonged to someone else. I looked at all the dust and refuse that had gathered round my feet – old coke cans, inflated newspaper sheets, cigarette butts, a puddle of dirty water – and I began to feel stuck. I wondered how I came to be in this position in the first place.

I could not relate to the accounts of the anorexic girl I saw circulated in some critiques of media images of beauty: the naive adolescent with the "reading disorder", the impressionable, uncritical consumer of fashion spreads. Nonetheless, I acted with the knowledge that as a young woman I always teetered dangerously near social unaccept-ability. I often imagined that I was wearing a flashing sign, an advertisement that broadcast to the world the worth and the size of me. As I interpreted the situation, I was responsible for the upkeep of the segments of my life which were arranged like the numbered features in a woman's magazine: first Beauty, then Career, then Relationships. The project was to make oneself over, playing by rules that required hourly reinforcement: Look yourself up and down; Watch what you eat, Check what you say and do in public; Don't take up too much time and space; Don't grow out your body hair. And most crucially: Don't be too much – too emotional, outspoken or aggressive, don't be fat and noticeable, don't be too loud.

But if, as a seventeen-year-old, I was burdened by round-the-clock self-vigilance, if I was even beginning to resemble the marketer of some new soft drink with my particular concerns about maintaining a controlled, well-researched appearance, then I never once spoke about my affliction. The philosophy I adopted as a young anorexic woman implicitly downgraded female preoccupation with body and any differences made by gender. It said: be self-contained;

be pure as the mind; be as successful as a man. Thus, I hid from view the starved, exhausted body, and the weight-obsessed mind that were the by-products of an appearance of androgynous independence. I disapproved of all policies of affirmative action, even as I envied men who seemed to be guided by a great caressing hand that pushed them up the slope. I chose to rely instead on inner strength and individual self-responsibility of the type that Helen Garner has boasted:

> *My friends and sisters and I . . . got ourselves through decades of being wolf-whistled, propositioned, pestered, insulted, attacked and worse without the big guns of sexual harassment legislation to back us up. [We took] it like . . . women – not like wimps who ran to the law to whinge about some minor unpleasantness instead of standing up and fighting back* (1995, p. 40).

What occurs to me now re-reading Garner is the degree to which my anorexia was fostered by the best liberal ideals: power in the individual, self-sufficiency, and the will to achieve, to be a competitor among formal equals in the marketplace. These were the "post-feminist" values, after all, that were routinely held up as available to individuals of both genders when I was a teenager. I adhered to them, never feeling sufficiently confident to question or contest the goals and hindrances I had been socially assigned. Instead, I accepted it was natural that I should feel my world was set to fall apart unless I lost a certain amount (of weight, of extravagance). And, when anorexia came, I listened without arguing to various medical accounts of the genesis of my perplexing pathology. In the doctor's surgery, I nodded my head placidly in time to the psychiatric narrative that explained my immaturity, my inability to ride through conflict on my bicycle, Garner-style. I read up on the psychoanalytic story that depicted me as a nervy and female Peter Pan who had chosen to shirk femininity and abrogate adult sexuality and responsibilities.

Of course, I always knew as a teenager that excessive body-consciousness for women made perfect sense in the marketplace. I understood that anorexia was the logical accompaniment to a myth which had personal and professional successes circling like a replica of the Miss World crown around a perfected female body. But it is only now, five years after my experience of emaciation, that I have really been able to reject the standard version of anorexia as a mysterious and atypical psychopathology. Moreover, it is only now that I am able to interrogate the liberated context in which I starved myself. My decision to speak about eating disorders is, as I have said, in part a decision to combat the cultural imperative that decrees anorexia as something to be overcome and attributed to female vanity. But it is also a response to the litany of comments that have been made in the context of the sexual harassment debate, about the perceived need for young women to take individual responsibility for the effects of their bodies in the world. Again, it is perhaps Garner who captures the flavour of these remarks, arguing that women must be continually awake to their "erotic . . . self-presentation" (1995, p. 89). She asks:

> *Can a young woman really expect to go through life without having to take this sort of responsibility?* (1995, p. 89).

Today I find myself enraged by the "get real" antagonism of Garner's question. If nothing else, I am astounded by her move to "return" responsibility for self-presentation back to women. For what, I want to shout, is the woman with an eating disorder doing if not accepting the onus to watch herself and be responsible for her self-presentation all the time? When I was seventeen, I memorised all the laws that existed about how bodies should look and I stayed gloriously obedient to them. I never got to ask, as Margaret Atwood does in her novel *Lady Oracle* (1972) just why the fat body undressing should be called obscene, or why emaciation equals emancipation. Instead, I believed that I had to accept the fact that it was dangerous to own or expose too much flesh. And I remembered the drone of a certain statement of my childhood: "The world's not going to change".

I am no longer prepared for the world not to change. Or to put the proposition another way, I don't see why women should have to change and starve and evacuate and contain their bodies in order to please the world. I am no longer prepared to ignore or glide over the differences that my gender has made to my experiences in the world. Clearly, the memory of anorexia still pulls and prods me, and maybe it also exposes cracks in the edifice of the liberal-feminist world view. These after all, are the origins of my understanding of feminism right now: a dissatisfaction with the post-feminist mentality of the competitive marketplace, of the schools I attended and the magazines I read in my teens. My feminism has come from a realisation that a declaration of inner strength and invincibility, a sharp profile in the mirror and the dropping of digits on the scales, are not tantamount to equality and freedom. I cannot and will not live by the adage that "less is more".

Generation (Se)X

Anita Harris

Before I explain how Henry Rollins made me a virgin, I'll tell a small story. When I was twelve years old, one of my best friends, a boy, asked me to be his girlfriend. We were already good mates, we talked into the night and slept over at each other's place, so what was supposed to change? Why did we suddenly need a shift in status? I declined the offer, mostly because I didn't know what it would entail. I had no idea what girlfriends did, but I wasn't much inclined to be part of it.

However, at some point in my youth, I chose not to be lesbian (as much as a choice for the status quo can ever be called a choice). This decision meant that I found myself in the dominant culture's organisation of sexual relations. After all, there is no denying that heterosexuality is our culture's only sexual reality; that its privilege is invisible and its exact nature is generalised. In short, it is the norm. How I became heterosexual is less clear to me; although, like becoming a woman, it was and remains a process that was both guided and self-generated. And while the process of becoming heterosexual certainly wasn't all bad, it also wasn't freely chosen from a full range of equally available sexual options. At any rate, by the time I was nineteen, I was a heterosexual feminist who incidentally liked punk rock. Heterosexuality seemed easier to negotiate via an alternative milieu such as punk rock because this scene grappled with the problems of social rules.

During this time, I went to hear American punk icon, Henry Rollins, do a spoken-word performance in Melbourne. One story he told was about a one-night-stand with a young college student. He described the attractiveness of this young woman, and how they went back to her room to have sex. Some time into intercourse, she changed her mind, pushed him off her and fell asleep. To get revenge, to get back at her for making him feel horny and not doing anything about it (he told the crowd), he jerked off on her beautiful clean hair while she slept, and then left. Most men in the audience laughed. I felt devastated. In my naive way, I separated the independent music scene from mainstream sexism. I wanted to believe that people – men – who thought critically about the world and who were committed to social justice were also open to feminism. And some of them were, especially on the surface. However, when it came to sex, it was obvious that politics wasn't the priority. The punk subculture was no more radical than the social order it claimed to react against. This got me thinking, not only about the place of women in alternative politics, but also about what heterosexuality means for young people across subcultures, and where this leaves young heterosexual feminists.

These memories aren't the only ones I have about heterosexuality, nor are they intended to tell the whole story. Rather, they illustrate two central elements of the patriarchal model of heterosexuality that we, as young women are meant to learn. First, we are supposed to abide by pre-existing rules about girlfriends and boyfriends and how we are supposed to relate and behave together. Developing creative, alternative relationships between the sexes is difficult because they fall outside the rules. And secondly, heterosex is supposed to be about the exercise of masculinity and dominance. Henry Rollins' self-congratulatory sexual act captured this in action.

However, I also have teenage memories of relationships and sexual experiences with boys that were about respect, tenderness, openness, mutuality, laughter and "equality-lust". While these are not the dominant images of heterosexuality, they should be. These days, it is important for me to rethink heterosexuality along these lines, to divest it of violence, man-making and myth-making, and to understand how my heterosexuality might fit with my feminism. I became heterosexual the way most people do, but I can now also make decisions about how to live this. It has become clear to me that sex and sexuality are not private concerns, but rather rule-bound, and currently women do not set the rules. Dominant forms of heterosexuality – models which highlight women's functionality and position as objects – reinforce men's power over women.

Our common understandings about heterosexuality are based on an acceptance of a fundamental difference between the social groups of women and men. This difference is generally an unequal one, and this inequality is eroticised. Heterosexuality (hetero meaning other) is about the frisson of hierarchical difference, where men are supposed to achieve their sexual selves by constructing women as the Other. For boys to become successful heterosexual men, they must learn to participate in the sexual objectification of women. In this light, I see my youthful lack of interest in heterosex as reasonable. While I hardly had an articulate feminism in my teens, I did have a sense of what was at stake in the traditional heterosexual relationship. My fear that for women, dominant forms of heterosexuality spell loss of self was confirmed by my late teens.

I am interested in radical heterosexuality that instead allows women to gain self in relationships with men. This approach regards both sexuality and subjectivity[1] (and the links between them) as human potentials rather than male prerogatives. In fact, the heterosexuality I envisage wouldn't really live up to its nomenclature, because it would be a sexuality between people, not genders. As such, it would move beyond a sexual relation of differently valued opposites and become an intimacy and a knowing between two whole, equal selves. There would still be genitals, but they would be attached to whole bodies. There would still be desire, but it would come with a complex web of emotions. In short, our whole subjectivity would become a central part of our heterosexual connections, instead of the liability it

---

1   A sense of independent identity or selfhood.

currently is. We would no longer aim to lose ourselves in hetero-relations, as is the popular image of women in love (or in bed) with men. Rather, our sense of self would be integral to this intimacy.

I don't pretend to be the first heterosexual feminist to have thought these ideas, and I think it is important to draw strength from this history. Since the first wave, heterosexual feminists have responded to the challenge of realising alternative forms of heterosexuality that exist outside patriarchal constructions. There are many feminists whose heterosexuality has been about celebrating autonomy and agency, mutual recognition and respect. In short, a sexuality without dominance, submission and objectification. Some younger feminists today such as Rene Denfeld (1995) have dismissed these earlier feminists as "anti-sex" and laden down by Victorian moralism. Reading the words of Victoria Woodhull (1873/1992), Tennessee Claflin (1897), Bessie Harrison Lee (1903), Emma Goldman (1911/1972) and Elizabeth Cady Stanton (1922), it seems clear that they opposed male-defined sex and male-defined morals, and wanted in its place a heterosexuality that involved something other than just men's ejaculations, sexually transmitted diseases, unwanted pregnancies and continuous male access. To call this anti-sex is to accept the patriarchal under-standing of sex as definitive. Instead, these women attempt-ed to realise a form of sexuality outside male definitions.

What I want to do is take up the challenge that our fore-mothers have passed on. Marilyn Frye, has suggested that we rethink words as well as practices around sexual selfhood, to turn around the images and experiences of heterosexual women. The word "virgin" is particularly compelling. At high school, with the pressure bearing down on us to achieve ourselves as correctly adult and sexual within the patriarchal rules, this was about the worst label someone could wear. Now, and in part because of what this high school experience represents, I see "reconstructed virginity" as a thrilling possibility for heterosexual feminists. Frye writes:

> *The word "virgin" did not originally mean a woman whose vagina was untouched by any penis, but a free woman, one not . . . bound to, not possessed by any man. It meant a female who is sexually, and hence socially, her own person* (1992, p. 133).

Henry Rollins has convinced me that radical heterosexuality has a lot to gain from the possibilities of "woman-made virginity". He made me a virgin, not so much because I no longer wanted to have sex with men (although he hardly built a compelling case on this front), but because I know that my heterosexuality had to be free and uncolonised. Frye says that for heterosexual women today, the original meaning of virginity can be a radical concept and practice because "[w]hat must be imagined here are females who are willing to engage in chosen connections with males, who are wild, undomesticated females, creating themselves here and now" (1992, p. 134). She argues for *wilful* virginity, with heterosexual women being political, self-determining, and sexually autonomous in their relationships with men.

For me, this involves a number of things.[2] Firstly, a willingness to see the politics in heterosexuality, not just as

---

2 As with Marilyn Frye's "sketch" of wilful virgins (1992, p. 134) on which these ideas build, these notes towards radical heterosexuality are my own thoughts on the matter, and are not intended to be "rules".

an institution, but in everyday life. And then, to make a conscious commitment to work against these politics. This might range from rejecting marriage to ensuring a fair division of household duties. It might mean living in separate houses, or having separate rooms and valuing separate space. It certainly involves a refusal to accept any kind of physical, sexual or emotional use and abuse. Secondly, wilful virgins maintain a sense of self in their relationships with men. They continue to value relationships with others, especially women, while heterosexually involved. They understand themselves as independent human beings, even when in intimate partnership with others. They meet men face to face, in all their human dimensions, with flaws and strengths, and only accept relationships which allow this. They demand to be enriched, rather than diminished by heterosexuality. And thirdly, sexual autonomy is integral to wilful virginity. Fundamentally, this means knowing, loving and respecting your body as part of you, and bringing this knowledge, love and respect for yourself to heterosex. Wilful virgins don't derive pleasure from sexually objectifying themselves or being objectified by men. They might have loads of lusty, orgasmic, penetrative sex, or prefer kissing, tingling, just-touching sex. Whatever ways they do heterosex, and this includes not doing sex when they don't feel like it, they remain present as equal subjects with their partners.

Wilful virginity is not about purity or sexual morality, but self-actualisation. Being a virgin means a commitment to mutual recognition of personhood in heterosex and relationships with men. It has nothing to do with whether or not intercourse happens, but rather who is really "there" if it does. In other words, it means moving beyond the two rather limited possibilities of the fucker and the fucked, the initiator and the recipient, and beyond the pre-fabricated fantasies and roles offered to us through popular culture. It means respecting your feelings when you do not want sex, without suffering guilt or self-doubt, in spite of our culture pathologising such disinclinations. We are not "co-present" if we have sex for any reason other than emotionally and/or physically wanting to: our vaginas, mouths and hands are not gifts, promises, enticements or items with which to barter. Similarly, we are not co-present if sex makes us feel degraded, reluctant, regretful, detached from our bodies or, indeed, like cocky conquerors. And co-presence cannot occur if a third party – a fantasy of another person or a pornographic image – is in bed with us. Achieving this mutuality means resisting the desire to be a sexual subject at the expense of another, but also resisting the cosy niche created for women to experience their sexual identity through their own objectification. John Stoltenberg writes:

> *If there is ever to be any possibility of sexual equality in anyone's lifetime, it requires, minimally, both the capacity and the commitment to regard another person as a whole self, as someone who has an integrity of independent and autonomous experience, as someone who is, simply, just as real as oneself* (1990, p. 55).

Nett Hart adds:

> *If the one with whom you are sexual . . . is someone you know and who knows you, someone of whom you are not afraid, then it will be impossible to Objectify. We can welcome the whole package of who we are and who our partner is. We can both be Subjects, actively attentive* (1996, pp. 73–4).

I believe that this is possible, even with someone who we don't know, as long as we know that they are someone. As heterosexual women we need to grapple with our investment in the maintenance of subject/object sexuality. To my mind, this means abandoning the old rules and starting again. We need to think about how we learned hetero-sexuality, especially those of us whose education consisted of information about men's sexual "needs", the primacy of intercourse, "kissing practice" with other girls, and the mysterious absence of the clitoris from anatomy diagrams. We need to understand why it is so easy for us to accept the subject/object division in heterosexuality (because it seems so natural), and why we might perpetuate our own object-ification (because we are offered no other role in heterosexual-ity). Through an examination of the rules through which we learn heterosexuality, we can start to imagine other possibilities, and begin to include ourselves in the picture as knowledgeable, wilful (and resistant) protagonists, rather than as supporting roles to men.

I think this kind of analysis around heterosexuality is more urgent than ever, because it comes at a time when the debate threatens to be sidetracked by red herrings about generational feminism and interpretations of sex. Since Helen Garner's unhelpful analysis of young women's understanding of sexual harassment as a "mingy, whining, cringeing terror of sex" (1995, p. 193), we have been forced on to the defensive about our perspectives on hetero-sexuality. One approach is to take issue with the view that young women are anti-sex or, as Garner puts it, afraid of Eros. In answer to this attack, some young feminists have proclaimed themselves "bad girls".[3] Others argue that young

---

3 This term is in general usage, but in the context of this discussion, is most notably the title of Catharine Lumby's 1997 book, subtitled *the media, sex & feminism in the 90s.*

heterosexual feminists constitute a new wave because of different attitudes towards sexuality – we are Generation (se)X. Those who embrace the bad girl tag are keen to show that heterosexual women are sexual people, rather than a sexual absence or fearful of men. This is a reasonable pursuit and a feminist one, but I wonder why women are agreeing to define themselves using the patriarchal, dichotomous model of good/bad? For example, Naomi Wolf claims that her book *Promiscuities* "explore[s] the shadow 'slut' who walks alongside us as we grow up, sometimes jeopardising us and sometimes presenting us with a new sense of authentic identity; sometimes doing both at once" (1997, p. 7). The implication is that women's sexual authenticity can be found in the compelling, illicit and scary bad girl who lurks within. Wolf writes about young women who extol the virtues of male bodies, intercourse, penises, and affairs with older men; all of which is fine, if not terribly challenging to the current order. She does not write of any form of heterosexuality outside this order, and this lack of vision, this willingness to accept the bad girl as the only possibility for female sexual autonomy, I find disappointing. I believe a better alternative can be found in rewriting the rules around heterosexuality and rethinking dichotomies which limit us.

According to Catharine Lumby and others, it is precisely because they aren't interested in "repressive" and "puritanical" judgements about sex that young women dissociate themselves with feminism today. Kathy Bail claims that "there is little sympathy for the anti-porn, anti-het-sex strand of feminist thought" (1996, p. 13). Lumby and Bail's arguments are sometimes based on the premise that girls need to reject a moralistic, virginal and judgemental approach to sex, and admit their own desires and fantasies. The solution is to be more sexual, express "inappropriate" desires, and refuse to be "nice". As Sheryn George proclaims, the idea is "to encourage other women to take those words like 'cunt' and 'slut' and 'dog' back; to say, 'Have sex, be a woman, be a bitch . . . '" (1996, p. 42). In my view, while the starting points of these arguments may have been as noble and fundamentally feminist, they have become derailed along the way to the destination of female sexual autonomy.

Braver solutions emerge for women when we examine the representation and restrictions on female heterosexuality in the context of the system of patriarchy. Heterosexual women must be able to define their own sexuality, but they cannot do this within the terms set by patriarchy. If feminists seek an end to these terms, it makes no sense to turn to patriarchal labels, such as the slut, and celebrate them as the only true answers to oppression. Instead, we need to dismantle the system of labelling, calling the categories themselves into question. I am not convinced by the argument that using the bad girl tag is part of a feminist reclamation and redefinition of pejorative words like dyke, spinster and hag. This is unlikely to have ironic resonance outside an individual clique. Proclaiming oneself to be a slut, wearing "sluttish" clothes and treating gropes as flattery are all acts of dubious sardonic worth for they are surely lost in a patriarchal culture that is forged on this same representation of women (see Berg: 1996). The significance of reclaiming these words is that they are originally intended to punish those who lie outside the hetero-patriarchal laws of desire. But bad girls are not beyond these laws. In fact, they are integral to them. It is by labelling and dividing female sexuality into good and bad, naughty and nice, that patriarchy controls women's sexual identities. Saying "I'm a slut and proud of it" is continuous with patriarchy's tired old line that women are "really desperate for it": good girls pretend that they're not, and bad girls accept that they are. Simply deciding that "bad" is the better of the "good" or "bad" options does nothing to undo the system which establishes and renders these options meaningful. For every bad girl, there must also be good girls. Thus the system remains the same, but you've privileged yourself and left your sisters out to dry.

Fifteen years ago Roberta Sykes (1984) reminded white feminists that calls for sexual liberation were offensive to Koori women, who were still fighting for the right to be free of sexualising labels and treatment. Are we still refusing to listen to indigenous women? We also need to think about working-class women who are already subjected to over-surveillance by the state because of assumptions about their supposed promiscuity.[4] Set against this reality, I'm not sure that the bad girl is really capturing the range and complexity of young women's heterosexualities. In an attempt to resist other people's representations and to exercise some power of our own, we may have missed opportunities to think carefully

---

4 Those involved with the management of young working-class women, such as social workers, educators, health care providers, police officers and case managers often perpetuate these assumptions and treat these women as though they are sexually irresponsible and out of control. This occurs through classist administration of sex education and con-traception, sexual health checks, judgements about young (especially single) mothers, the differing treatment of rich and poor victims of sexual violence, and the policing of young working-class women for public behaviour deemed "inappropriate". See Griffin (1993) for an international perspective on this trend.

and creatively about heterosexuality. I don't know that we really want to be "bad". I think we want to be *free* – free of judgements, labels, reputations, sexual evaluations, pressure, coercion, violations of our sexual autonomy.

Some will argue that feminists like myself want all women to renounce heterosexuality, and only participate in boring, safe, "vanilla" sex, rejecting penetration as an act of domination. This is not my vision of the only feminist heterosexuality. I am quite sure that there will be orgasms after the revolution, and that some of these will happen in situations of lust without love, via intercourse, maybe from one-night stands – but they will be in circumstances of respect and recognition. My argument is not with specific forms of heterosexual practice *per se*, but the order of meanings that structure these practices and inform our behaviours. It is this limited repertoire that we need to resist by thinking critically about the ways it is imposed upon us and by refusing its enticements. It is crucial to recognise that women have always been defined by patriarchy as available for sex: the existence of pornography and prostitution makes it quite clear that patriarchy loves sluts. Resisting this definition is likely to bring more creative possibilities that embracing it.

I don't consider it very uplifting to imagine myself stalked by my shadow slut, creeping along behind me like a grubby man in a raincoat. This image evokes a sexuality of secret smut. I'd rather picture a liberated, shining symbol for radical heterosexuality, something flying free, compelling us forward into new possibilities. I imagine a guardian angel, a sort of wilful virgin trapeze artist with wings, operating outside the patriarchal order of bad/nice. As wilful virgin aerialists, we can fly above the ground rules, and use our bird's eye view to see alternatives to those two choices.

Real freedom comes from ending male control of sexuality, including the organisation of sexuality around subjects and objects. Real freedom also requires women's self-actualisation beyond patriarchy. This means being co-present, as an autonomous, whole self in relationships and sex with men. Becoming a "virgin" is a way to begin rethinking heterosexuality. Virgins gain rather than lose themselves in heterosexuality, because they demand recognition and self determination. They are sexual people who seek an "intimacy of equals" (Mohin, 1996). They fly in the face of sexual stereotypes and defend themselves against sexual colonisation. They understand the privilege and the problems of a heterosexual identity, and they work for sexual autonomy for all women. Marilyn Frye says, "to embody and enact a consistent and all-the-way feminism, you have to be a heretic, a deviant, an undomesticated female, an impossible being. You have to be a Virgin." (1992, p. 136). I am pleased to be developing a propensity for virginity, that is, for going all-the-way. Who would have thought that I'd have Henry Rollins to thank?

"Girlie Duco":
Notes on Fem(me)inism[*]

Galina Laurie

1990. I am nineteen. I live in an all-female residential college, whose residents think "feminism" is, paradoxically, a dirty word. I work on *Growing Strong*, Sydney University's women's information handbook. I am summoning up the courage to join the women's collective, worried that because I have long hair and don't own a boiler suit, I'll have no cred. I feel confused, caught between an anti-feminist "home" and the beginnings of a feminist conscious-ness. For the first time, I have the language to articulate

---

[*] Pat Gillespie used the phrase "girlie duco" in her witty discussion of toenail painting, published in *The Weekend Australian* (1998, p. 11).

my proto-feminist ideas. For the first time, I am around women who openly express their sexuality in *all* its manifestations. A dyke I know writes an essay about lipstick lesbians and the appropriation of a lesbian aesthetic by the straight media. I fall in love with one of my best friends: it's a disaster. I am too scared to wear skirts in case they are misread; my trousered, French-perfumed body already complicated by the fact that it can't walk like a boy. I am haunted by the whispers which seek to predict, proscribe and contain: "When will she cut her hair? What kind of a lesbian will she become?"

Women's Studies III: "The Question of Patriarchy". One morning in class it occurs to me that I have never wanted to piss standing up, unlike most of the other dykes in the seminar. We spend hours talking about power and difference, fisting and sadomasochism. I am living a feminist utopia, with a group of fellow students – friends – who are as curious as me. I am an "out" lesbian, having my first love affair of any kind. We have politically correct sex, initially without penetration. I read about *Wicked Women* – the Sydney-based movement of sex-radical dykes who stage performances and parties which explore gender-fuck – and wonder how to meet women like this. The love affair ends. I become the lover of the woman who will break my heart, after she has introduced me to S/M sex. I move house, and learn from my gorgeous femme, feminist flatmate how to wear a mean frock.

1998. I'm nearly twenty-eight and I'm having a fashion crisis. This is the summer of the strappy sandal. Until now, boots have been the way I queer the femininity of the frocks I like to wear. My feet are the last frontier, so giving up boots is my final capitulation to girliness. Watching my nude feet, toenails sparkling in the girlie duco of their polish, is not simply an autoerotic pleasure. Like all fashion crises, it's the combinations which cause trouble. This time, however, I'll have to look further than my clothes rack. I want to make sense of the seemingly uneasy relationship between different aspects of my identity: lesbian, feminist, femme. "I long to be smartly turned out for this femme reckoning, up on all the right theories, able to model that I'm a right-on white girl, that I am down with the lesbo/homo cause . . ." (Rugg: 1997, p. 175). I want to insist on femme as an authentic place from which to speak not only lesbian, but feminist.

What does it mean to "look like a girl"? As a femme, I have a history. A history which includes derision from lesbian feminists who saw butch-femme roles as anathema to their project of sexual liberation (McCowan: 1992; Medhurst: 1997; Pratt: 1997). Lesbian feminism is often re-membered as enacting the slogan: "feminism is the theory; lesbianism is the practice". What lesbian feminism effectively did was foreground the political potential of lesbian identity, by insisting that being a lesbian necessarily involved rejecting heterosexual models of sexuality. This included rejecting the idea of "sex roles". Under this rubric, butch-femme was seen a mimicry of male-female roles, and was, in the words of Rita Mae Brown, the quintessential lesbian feminist novelist, "the craziest, dumbass thing I ever heard tell of" (1973, p. 130). Lesbian feminism is also mistakenly marked as a mainly middle-class and white phenomenon, as against butch-femme which is frequently working class and multi-raced. I think that it is important to remember the raced, classed nature of debates around feminism and sexuality. Moreover, I want to know what it means when a "bourgie North Shore bitch" like myself participates in femme play.

As a femme, I confound my mother's expectations of what a lesbian looks like. Mum thought she had it sorted when I came out to her – *she* knew already because I didn't shave my legs or under my arms. But I played with dolls. In fact, I made my little brother play dolls too. Now, my frocking up seems to get her hopes up, but in all the wrong directions! I think she's conflated my feminist refusal to capitulate to the masculine desire for a hairless female body, with evidence of deviant sexuality. Perhaps for her, though, feminism and deviant sexuality aren't terribly far apart.

As a femme, I risk incurring scorn from straight feminists whose trouser-wearing often exceeds my own, and who see this as, strangely, upsetting an expected order. I risk contempt from dykes who can't see me, or who see my dyke identity as tenuous, available for heterosexual cooption at the bat of an eyelash. Other whispers haunt me now, speculating about the likelihood of a "turn" towards heterosexuality, selling out, sleeping with the enemy. This from butches, who herein reveal a belief that femme is not far enough away from the conventional femininity which they have fought so hard to escape.

I like the butch relocation of femininity, shifting it to a place which can be inhabited comfortably and erotically. I like the "dissonant juxtaposition and the sexual tension" produced when "masculinity, if it can be called that, is . . . brought into relief against a culturally intelligible 'female body'" (Butler: 1990, p. 123). For my lover, my femme desire is "a queer gender desire, not a desire for masculinity in any old body" (Harris and Crocker: 1997a, p. 97). But I don't think boydykes have dibs on playing with gender: I too like the sexiness of a floating signifier. The misreading involved in "passing" turns *me* on as much as it does her. If butch is butch because it recontextualises and resignifies masculinity in a girl's body, femme is not simply a falling towards heterosexuality.

She's a boy. My femme-ininity titillates her, which gives me courage to take it further.

"D'you think I could pass for straight?" I ask her. Holding my breath, convincing her (and me) that a positive answer is okay. She's squirming I can see, wondering how she will get out of this one alive.

"Yes, to straights, but not to dykes." I breathe again, but am not convinced.

If we are mimics, might it be unacceptable that we perform these roles ever so much better than heterosexuals?

I want something more complex, not to mention less judgemental, than lesbian feminism, butches, or my mother are prepared to offer. A reconfigured history of femme requires this, given that femmes also fought for women's rights throughout the history of twentieth-century feminism and sexual liberation. My own belief in feminist possibilities and queer choices necessitates reconciliation between these different aspects of my identity. I won't have my desire to play with power and gender dissed by feminists or lesbians who see me as blindly reinscribing an unreconstructed idea of femininity. I want such play to be seen as empowering me through my refusal to "conflate desire with political practice", (Harris and Crocker: 1997b, pp. 3–4) as negotiation, not ignorance of power and its workings.

Femme does not simply reinstate hetero-normative femininity. Rather, it is a reshaped femininity, one which is "transgressive, disruptive and chosen" (Harris and Crocker: 1997b, p. 3). It means naming femme as an identity I want to embrace. It means redeploying the frock, complicating it, troubling it as a queer signifier of femininity. It means that one way of living the freedoms promised and gained through feminism is to dress as I choose. If femme desire is not simply constituted within butch-femme relationships, and if I am more than the sum of my wardrobe's contents, then exactly "what kind of solitary pose will signify femme as independently lesbian?" (Rugg: 1997, pp. 177–8). Moreover, how might femme be readable as feminist? The problem with femme, it would seem, is one of readability.

I want to approach the question elliptically by proposing that the notion of femme community is an alternative to the butch-femme dyad and the solitary femme pose. What would the collective noun be, I wonder? A fan of femmes? A giggle of girl-dykes? Certainly a can of worms. Femme is not simply about fucking: it is also about femmes recognising each other; about femmes forming strong and lasting relationships.

There is a version of lesbian history which claims that femmes, unlike butches, had no community. According to oral histories of American butch-femme communities in the 1940s and 1950s, "[f]ems might have had individual girlfriends, but there was no network of fem friendship akin to the camaraderie of butches. Instead, there was a tradition of competitiveness" (Kennedy: 1997, p. 24).[2] I don't want to discredit this historical assertion, sceptical though I may be about its veracity, tempted though I may be to read it as misogyny relocated to a lesbian context. I do, however, want to contest the idea that femme-femme interactions necessarily take the form of catfights.

Some of my best friends are femmes – statement which doesn't hold much water, no matter how true it is. As a femme among femmes, I am recognisable, playful, at home. A fashion crisis shared is a fashion crisis halved . . . Feminism insists on the validity of communities of women, that such communities provide strength, passion, a sense of belonging. The femmes I know are smart, stroppy, ironic, mischievous – just the kind of woman I want to be. We are feminists too, fuelled by the desire to change the world. Frocks don't hamper our political commitment, nor, unlike our suffragette precursors, are they worn to give the appearance of proper femininity, to compensate for other breaches of feminine behaviour (Benson and Esten: 1996, p. 12). Like camping.

Mabel Maney, writer and (self-styled?) legendary femme was told, when she came out, that "[y]ou can't be a lesbian unless you like to camp" (Maney: 1997, p. 76). She argues that her femininity made her unrecognisable as a dyke in the eye of *that* beholder, a femininity in which her penchant for glamour is compounded by her dislike of outdoor pursuits. By way of contrast, some of the best camping trips I've ever been on have been in the company of my favourite femmes, with and without frocks. Apart from suggesting that enjoying "the great outdoors" is the sole prerogative of the less-than-femme, Maney's words foreground another meaning of camp which I like.

---

2 These oral histories were based on research conducted by Kennedy and Madeline Davis. *Boots of Leather, Slippers of Gold: The History of Lesbian Community* (Kennedy and Davis: 1994) looks at lesbian bar culture in Buffallo, New York, in the 1940 and 1950s.

My femmes and I, we like to *camp it up*. Camp in this sense is most often located within the domain of male homosexuality (Newton: 1972; Meyer: 1994; Medhurst: 1997). The screaming queen, the drag queen, Judy Garland as gay icon, and Oscar Wilde are all examples of camp. Andy Medhurst insists that this is where the buck stops: camp is "the way *gay men* have tried to rationalise, reconcile, ridicule and . . . wreck their own specific relationships with masculinity and femininity" (Medhurst: 1997, p. 291, my emphasis), and as such it defies appropriation into other arenas. I disagree. While recognising camp's political power and playfulness as historically specific, I want to extend its ambit by focusing on the queerness of camp: camp as "the total body of performative practices and strategies used to enact a queer identity, with the enactment defined as the production of social visibility" (Meyer: 1997, p. 5).

If femme entails "a set of behaviours used as codes" (Harris and Crocker: 1997b, p. 3), it is remarkably evocative of camp as performative practice and strategy. In the late nineties, dykes and feminists alike are frocking up, and I don't believe that this is a sign of post-feminism. Rather, it's a sign of powerful play, of defiance and pleasure. Feminism has given us all the possibility of contesting femininity, as well as the choice of how to do it. For me, putting on a frock or some polish contributes to the production of myself as consciously, critically and visibly femme. Femme is my queer feminist identity.

Generationalism:

The Ties That Bind

Mothers, Daughters, Sisters

Louise D'Arcens

Certain aspects of my behaviour seemed to have an immediate effect on my mother, an effect which had not the slightest connection with what I had intended. But between my sister and myself things happened naturally. We would disagree, she would cry, I would become cross, and we would hurl the supreme insult at one another: "You fool!" and then we'd make it up. Her tears were real, and if she laughed at one of my jokes, I knew she wasn't trying to humour me. She alone endowed me with authority . . .

SIMONE DE BEAUVOIR: 1959, PP 44–5.

To me, feminism has meant a range of things. In theory, it is a political position through which women struggle for recognition and rights. It challenges dominant assumptions about women, and it advocates increasing women's influence in the public sphere.

In practice, I regard everyday life as a feminist to be fundamentally a quest for authority. By this, I do not simply mean a search for economic power, corporate influence, or sway over government. Rather, for me, feminist authority is about women authorising themselves: believing in and valuing themselves, and giving legitimacy to their own perspectives as women – but also, importantly, to other women. It is individually enacted, but reflects a commitment to the empowerment of women in general.

My concern with feminist authority has grown out of my scholarly interests as well as my allegiance to feminism. Researching the theme of authority in the writings of late-medieval women, I have been inspired by the many ways in which these women found – or invented if necessary – strategies for authorising themselves. This did not simply entail establishing their own authorship, but also articulating feminine perspectives in a period marked by entrenched misogyny. As a feminist living in the 1990s, I am heartened by the ways in which women continue to seek out, redefine, and, crucially, act on their own authority in a climate increasingly characterised by backlash against the reforms achieved by feminists. While medieval and modern women have responded to vastly different circumstances, their shared endurance and resourcefulness bear witness to the persistence of women's struggle for self-determination.

My interest in feminist authority has drawn me to the highly publicised debates between older and younger Australian feminists over the past three years, especially those ignited by the publication of Helen Garner's controversial "faction", *The First Stone* (1995). Although this dialogue has spanned issues as varied as sexual harassment, law reform, women's status within professional and educational spaces, and the ethical hotbed of personal desire, the common theme throughout is an abiding concern with feminist authority. This involves a reconsideration not only of the authority of feminist politics within contemporary Australian culture, but also, at the most profound level, of the distribution of authority within Australian feminism itself: who has it, who wants it, and over whom.

Because age is the main axis of the struggle for authority in these debates, it is not surprising that commentators repeatedly draw upon the metaphor of generational conflict. In this scenario, older women are portrayed as feminist mothers, while younger women are their chronological and political daughters. It is this familial metaphor that is my primary concern, for I believe that it has not only determined the shape and direction of these debates, but it captures Australian feminists' conceptions of their own shifting authority.

Concentrating on feminists' use of metaphor rather than their discussion of concrete issues might at first seem somewhat rarefied. However, my study of medieval women's texts has convinced me that far from being abstract or merely incidental, metaphors have long been used by women as powerful tools of self-understanding. Fifteenth-century French writer Christine de Pizan is exemplary in this regard. In her famous debate with the masculine intellectuals of her day, called the *Débat sur le Roman de la Rose* (*Quarrel of the Rose*, 1978), she conceptualised herself as a *petite point de ganivet*, a "small dagger point" that punctures the "bulging sack" of masculine erudition that had traditionally served to denigrate women. Elsewhere, her image of herself as an *architectus* or "master-builder" allowed her to "build" her proto-feminist utopian text of 1405, *Le Livre de la Cité des Dames* (*The Book of the City of Ladies*, 1982). In a comparable way, Australian feminists metaphorising themselves as mothers and daughters determine not only how we see ourselves, but also how we interact with one another and the kinds of authority we grant each other. Ultimately, how we describe ourselves defines – and circumscribes – the forms of agency we can exercise. Metaphors are not simply about semantics, but have practical implications for the ways in which women act.

Australian feminism of the 1990s was initially – and most notoriously – described as a mother-daughter conflict by Helen Garner in *The First Stone*, an account Anne Summers described in the *Good Weekend* as a "maternal lament" (1995, p. 28). Garner's book is replete with references to intergenerational warfare and alienation. Her clearest portrayal of herself as a rejected feminist mother is found in her account of a strained encounter with Melbourne University's Women's Officer:

> *So, this is about middle-aged mothers and daughters, then . . .*
> *I was her political mother, and she was busily, calmly, coldly,*
> *demolishing me . . .* (1995, pp. 97–8).

Without detailing all the permutations of Garner's use of the mother-daughter conflict model, it is worth briefly stating that in *The First Stone* and other articles and interviews, she presents young women as shrill, oversubtle "punitive girls"(1995, p.100), whose litigious puritanism and fixation on their own juridical disempowerment marks their departure from their political mothers' radical libertarian feminism – a departure narrated by Garner as an act of filial ingratitude and disrespect. By presenting young women in this way, Garner also implicitly condemns the 1990's feminism that she sees embodied in them. On the other side of this conflictual paradigm, Garner presents the image of the progressive mother, whose worldly experience has made her sceptical of the law, and attuned to the unpredictable "dance" of Eros in everyday life.

In spite of her often alarmingly broad strokes, Garner's archetypal portrait of feminism as a mother-daughter

conflict has impeccable feminist credentials. Indeed, disobedience toward the mother has been the progressive
woman's rite of passage for centuries. In *The Book of the City
of Ladies* we find Christine de Pizan recounting how she
gained an education in spite of her mother's "feminine
opinion", which restricted her activities to "spinning and
silly girlishness"(1982, pp.154–5). This pattern continued
for a number of centuries in Europe, with educated women
regularly pointing to their mothers as the greatest obstacle
to their intellectual ambition. More recent instances of this
can be found in the work of second-wave feminism's own
intellectual "mother", Simone de Beauvoir. In her autobiog-
raphical *Memoirs of a Dutiful Daughter* (1959), she describes
the gradual shift from childhood symbiosis with her mother
to adolescent alienation – an account which she echoes on
a philosophical level in *The Second Sex* when she writes:

> *Real conflicts arise when the girl grows older . . . she wishes to
> establish her independence from her mother. This seems to
> the mother a mark of ingratitude; she tries obstinately to
> checkmate the girl's will to escape* (1971, p. 534).

In *The Second Sex*, de Beauvoir offers an interesting explanation of this kind of maternal authoritarianism when she
discusses the narcissistic nature of the mother's relation to
her daughter – that is, her desire to see herself reflected in
the person of her daughter. De Beauvoir says:

> *In her daughter, the mother . . . seeks a double. She projects
> upon her daughter all the ambiguity of her relation with
> herself; and when the otherness of this alter ego manifests
> itself, the mother feels herself betrayed* (1971, p. 532).

In a twist, Garner reverses the traditional conflictual

paradigm in the sense that for her, it is the mothers rather than the daughters who are progressive. She nevertheless frames her own sense of alienation from younger feminists within the terms of this same paradigm.

It is, I believe, because of its feminist pedigree, rather than its accuracy, that Garner's mother-daughter paradigm has proven so compelling. Her argument brings with it an historical weight and seductive familiarity that renders it difficult to resist. And, indeed, few have resisted. While a number of the more virulent critics of Garner's own generation have disputed her jaundiced view of young women, conspicuously few – until the recent publication of the important essay collection *bodyjamming* (1997)[1] – questioned the accuracy or usefulness of her familial metaphor as a description of contemporary Australian feminism. Now, as the debate moves through its newest stage, with younger (and older) feminists publicly rebutting the charges levelled against young women by Garner and her supporters, the time has come to halt the momentum of the story of generational conflict.

Two of the more comprehensive responses from young Australian feminists have been journalist Virginia Trioli's exhaustively researched *Generation f* (1996) and Kathy Bail's pop-anthology *DIY Feminism* (1996). While Trioli argues convincingly that young women continue to be committed to social reform, Bail's book attempts to map contemporary feminism's transition from an older, "dowdy" form of collective resistance to a new, "sassy" brand of individualist lifestyle politics. However, while these texts

---

1   For criticisms of generationalism in this collection see XX's "Sticks and Stones", Foong Ling Kong's "Outlaws in a Jam", and Ann Curthoys' "Where is Feminism Now?"

offer some important and subtle correctives to Garner's archetypal story, they still define their position within the terms of her generation-gap myth.[2]

Bail, for instance, opens *DIY Feminism* with an unquestioning affirmation of the "generational shift" taking place in contemporary feminism, coining the term "femme gen" to describe the diffuse body of twentysomething women who make up her feminist constituency. Furthermore, while the concept of "DIY" implies an anarchic, self-generated style of feminism, Bail nevertheless frames it in terms of daughterly disobedience in the face of narcissistic feminist mothers who, she says, "are . . . searching for a younger, easily recognisable version of themselves. [But] there aren't many dutiful daughters" (1996, p. 3). *DIY* contributors refer to the possibility that "jealous mothers" rank among "femme gen's" critics. Finally, Bail's occasionally laboured emphasis on "fun" as the hallmark of young feminism, although valuable as a riposte to Garner's caricature of young women as "priggish", risks casting young feminists in the role of adolescent daughters dissociating themselves from a nagging maternal "culture of complaint".

These responses inadvertently draw our attention to an important pitfall in debates deploying the generational model. Because this model is based on an unequal, hierarchical relationship between successful middle-aged mothers and less established feminist daughters, inevitably discussions are less about feminist authority – whether personal or collective authority – and more about the authoritarian relationship between feminists of different ages. As we have

---

2 Another book worth mentioning in this context is Catharine Lumby's (1997) *Bad Girls* which, as the title suggests, takes up the motif of daughterly disobedience as characterising the feminist practices of young women.

seen, not only have older feminists launched parental diatribes in an attempt to control the politics of their dis-obedient daughters, but younger feminists have in turn formulated their own independence in terms of an adolescent rebellion against an oppressive and out-of-touch older generation. This raises the question of whether, within this model, it is possible for young feminists to respond to their elders without in some way reinforcing the predetermined image of insolent daughters.

Trioli's handling of what she calls "the supposed generational divide" is more searching, as she argues "the epochal change that is taking place in Australia is . . . a far more complex struggle" (1996, p. 9). However, the tension at the core of her account results from her desire to defend her generation while at the same time casting doubt upon the very concept of feminist generations. This is most apparent in her chapter entitled "Jealous Mothers". Here, she has recourse to the generational paradigm both in her question "[h]ow is a mother to feel when the daughter snatches greedily at treasure nurtured for her and then runs with it?" (1996, p. 149), and in her uncharacteristic generalisation of older feminists as the "smug generation . . . who believe they were the only ones to get that exquisite mix of sexual abandonment and self-definition absolutely right" (1996, p. 41).

This kind of statement reveals another major flaw in the mother-daughter model: its reliance on caricature. Indeed, at times the public debate degenerated not so much into mud-slinging as intellectual mud wrestling – a cartoon-like spectacle of female conflict staged for the benefit of a prurient anti-feminist spectatorship, rather than for the women involved. In particular, this model is open to criticism because it conveniently maps chronological age onto feminist progress – that is, if you are a certain age, you must embrace the form of feminism "appropriate" to that age. In order to draw battle lines, we stifle the diversity that exists between women, herding older and younger women into opposing camps. The effect of this is that all women in their fifties are assumed to share Garner *et al's* post-second-wave disillusionment with feminism, while the generic young feminist, based on a combination of the Garner and Bail stereotypes, becomes a curious hybrid figure who sits provocatively-dressed at her computer emailing her solicitor.

The tenuous assumptions on which this model is based can be exposed on several counts. To begin with, much of the acrimony that has passed between feminists has been between women of the same chronological generation – such as Garner and Australian writer Cassandra Pybus[3] – rather than between older and younger women. Furthermore, this model overlooks the fact that not all women become feminists in their youth. Indeed, to rework an old phrase, there's a feminist born every minute. Many women, for instance, whose age would place them in "the Garner generation" have only recently embraced feminist ideals in the wake of their (biological) daughters' involvement with the Movement. While these older women's 1990s' feminism might not entail the youthful accoutrements of

---

3   Interestingly, one of the issues that Garner and Pybus have differed over is the nature of the maternal role of older feminists. Their respective conceptions of feminist motherhood have differed significantly: Pybus' concept has been based more on the importance of protecting young women in their social and juridical vulnerability (Pybus: 1995), while Garner's is based on advising them to recognise, and deal responsibly with, their youthful power as "anima figures" (Garner: 1995, p. 89).

the "femme gen", neither will it necessarily subscribe to the radical libertarian ethic that is attributed to established older feminists.[4]

My own mother's story is an eloquent testimony to this. As a young home-maker with three small children in the late 1960s and early 1970s, she has told me that she felt not only disconnected from feminism, but in fact actively alienated and even denounced by its libertarian agenda. As an adolescent feminist, my relationship with my mother followed the progressive woman's established pattern, marked by my struggles to express my blazing nascent politics and her fearful attempts to prevent me from becoming one of those women whom, she believed, had condemned her in the past. The tension between us pivoted on a misunderstanding of one another's concept of feminist authority. Caught between an older feminism she feared and a younger feminism she did not recognise, my mother had a difficult negotiation process before her – far more difficult than my own, which was more akin to pondering how to unwrap some marvellous gift that seemed to have fallen from the heavens into my lap. Now in her fifties, my mother has developed her own form of feminist authority which, although it still bears the traces of her traditional caution about using the *f* word, is in many ways closer to my own than to the agenda of 1970s' feminism. She is yet to become a cyber-grrl (although her forays onto the internet have been less tentative than my own), and has not flirted extensively with sassy "bad-girl" feminism.

---

4 Ann Curthoys, in her astute argument in *bodyjamming*, offers a similar criticism of the alignment of age with style of politics, saying "what distinguishes women from one another is not their generation, but the timing of their exposure to feminist ideas" (1997, pp. 205–6).

Nevertheless she, like me, is a late beneficiary of the powerful legacy of 1970s' feminism, supporting women's demands for social justice and accepting their prerogatives to autonomy, enjoyment of their sexuality, and self-belief. We often joke together that while she is my biological mother, she is also my feminist daughter.

Having discussed this with my feminist friends, I realise that the situation I share with my mother is far from unique. Many of us, in a complicated drama of political inheritance, have brought our mothers to feminism, passing on our insights to them just as they passed, and continue to pass, theirs on to us. In replacing the model of generational conflict with one of intergenerational re-ciprocity, I am drawing on a metaphor with a pedigree even more ancient than that of maternal conflict, reaching back at least as far as the profound loyalty shared by Ruth and her cherished mother-in-law Sarah in the Old Testament Book of Ruth. Returning to *The Book of the City of Ladies*, Christine de Pizan offers the striking fable of a Roman woman who sustains her starving mother by breastfeeding her in prison. Praising the filial bond between them, Christine says "[i]n this way, the daughter gave back to her mother in her old age what she had taken from her mother as an infant" (p. 115). Although Christine's own relationship with her mother was more fraught, in this story we see her attempt to figure the mother-daughter relationship in a more egalitarian and non-conflictual way.

In my view it is time for us to turn to a different model of contemporary feminist authority than that offered by the mother-daughter paradigm. What is required is a model that can acknowledge the unavoidable conflicts between women while also recognising the more flexible, and less authoritarian nature of their relationships. One such model, already available within feminist terminology, is that of sisterhood.

Sisterhood has long functioned within feminist discourse as a crucial alternative to the patriarchal metaphor of the "brotherhood" of Man. In the context of the current debate, however, I believe that it can operate as an alternative to the divisive mother-daughter model. The kind of sisterhood I propose does not call up a sentimental ideal of harmony at the expense of acknowledging the often irreconcilable differences between women. Any model that evades the issue of feminist conflict – and here, I include Bail's attractive but glib DIY emphasis on diverse lifestyles – is inappropriate for contemporary Australian feminism, where issues such as ethnicity, socio-economic status, and sexual preference are just as much a source of productive tensions as age difference. On the contrary, as is demonstrated by Rosemary Neill's image of the "new guard . . . [who] are sick of being overshadowed by their self-serving baby-boomer sisters" (1995, p. 1), conflict is as much a part of sisterhood as harmony or shared interests. Older and younger sisters fight with each other and resent each other, sometimes bitterly.

Nevertheless, this model enjoys a number of advantages over the generational model. First of all, it does not privilege the axis of age difference over other forms of difference between women. Secondly, rather than a relationship of debt, in which the younger feminist owes it to the older feminist to maintain a continuous feminist vision, sisterhood stresses the idea of a shared inheritance. While there will inevitably be arguments about how to manage this inheritance, the important thing is that it belongs to everybody, to be valued and developed together. Thirdly, while it is undeniable that sisterhood has its own hierarchies, they are more flexible than the rigid hierarchy imposed by the mother-daughter relationship, in which chronology bestows authority upon one party alone, and with it, the prerogative of punishment. Describing ourselves according to this more flexible image is more than a question of semantic sleight-of-hand. By replacing a hierarchical metaphor with an image that approaches the idea of equality, we keep open the possibility of a dialogue between women that rigorously discusses differences – without losing sight of what is held in common.

I return to this metaphor because it has operated powerfully in my own life. Like many others I know, my mother and I have really struggled over the years to deal with our conflicts in a way that sidesteps the tired circuit of generational recriminations. For me, this has been possible through seeing her as both mother and sister. This has presented a special challenge, not only because of the entrenched nature of the mother-daughter conflictual paradigm, but in particular because as two biologically sisterless women, we have had to invent a model of sisterhood based on guesswork rather than experience. Nevertheless, I feel that in choosing to regard one another as sisters, we have managed to develop a sisterhood based on shared recognition rather than rivalry. This has certainly not prevented conflict arising between us; however, it has enabled us to strive as equals if not toward resolution then at least mutual tolerance of our differences.

Ultimately, it is counter-productive to see 1990s' feminism as an empire that is either falling prey to an adolescent *coup d'état* or covetously ruled over by rapacious matriarchs. Instead, sisterhood in its very simplicity, acknowledges the complexity of feminism as an overlapping series of actual lives and experiences rather than an abstract familial grid. Whether this conflictual sisterhood is described as a war or a dialogue, its flexibility ensures that while one authoritarian mother may have been quick to cast the first stone, it may well be authoritative – and, importantly, self-authorising – sisters who get the last word.

Sisters at Any Age

Ingrid McKenzie

So here I sit, thinking about my contribution to a book of young feminists' writing. I'm suddenly gripped by uncertainty. I am thirty-three. Can I still be called young at thirty-three?

I could answer that question in two ways. One response is that I am relatively young, especially when compared to the women who are visible in the Women's Movement today in Australia, although this is changing. Alternatively, my answer could be more defensive. I was in my twenties when I joined the Women's Electoral Lobby (WEL), and I certainly was perceived as young when I became WEL's National Coordinator at twenty-nine.

There are, however, more interesting questions to ask which shed light on the tensions between feminists – indeed women generally – of different ages. More important issues run parallel to my questions: Why am I anxious about whether I'm "young enough", and whether I'm the "right" age?

For almost as long as I can remember, no age ever seemed to be the "right" age. When I was about five, I remember wanting to be like my older sister and brother. They were bigger, and physically more able than me. They had more information and therefore knew more than I did, and they were treated differently. It seemed to me that my sister, brother and I were valued according to what and how much we knew about the world.

When I was a young teenager, I longed to reach the magical age of eighteen. At last I would be "there", I would be "legal" – recognised by the political and legal system as old enough to vote, drink alcohol and go to R-rated movies. When I was sixteen, I wondered what I would be doing at twenty-three. I imagined that by then I would be living a "real" life, as if somehow I wasn't already alive.

At twenty-one, I looked forward to my late twenties when I would really have things worked out, and when it appeared that age wouldn't matter as much. I would be finished with my formal education and out in the world "living". Life would begin when I graduated from university, was engaged in a career, and building expertise and confidence in my dealings with all aspects of society.

And now I'm thirty-three, and I find that I look both forward and back. I feel at once both too young and too old.

It is particularly in paid employment as a lawyer in the Commonwealth Public Service that I feel young. The feeling arises because I am sometimes treated differently from the way my older colleagues treat each other but also because the reality is that many of those with whom I work are at least ten years older than I am.

On the other hand, recently, I have been increasingly aware of being "too old", and I'm sure it will only grow stronger with years. I worry that others have achieved more by the time they reach my age, and that I'm so old that I can't get into today's clothing fashions. Increasingly, I am conscious of people younger than me. I notice them calling radio stations to request songs I have never heard of and others occupying positions of influence. This makes me insecurely question whether I could have achieved more by now.

It seems that a lot of my time and energy has been consumed with thoughts about the "right" age, with me wishing I was older or younger, never quite comfortable with exactly where I stood. And I'm sure I am not unique in having this preoccupation.

I see this preoccupation as a symptom of a broader pattern of oppression in society – oppression on the basis of age. Age oppression affects most of us growing up and living in Australia. It seems to me that an understanding of age oppression and its effects on women hasn't formed a significant part of the discussion about younger and older feminists that has raged for the last few years. Behind much of the debate there appears to be a lack of recognition of the dramatic effects of age oppression and the way that it, coupled with women's oppression, keeps women separated from one another. To overcome this division, we need to understand why it happens – talk about it, understand how it affects us and move toward building a unified feminist voice.

It has long seemed self-evident to me that young people are oppressed. Yet this view unfailingly stirs up very strong emotions, particularly when it is pat to those older than myself. The statement seems radical to them because older people face their own version of age oppression; to them, young people have it all, so why are they complaining?

For eighteen years, we do not control the critical decisions affecting our lives. While we still have much to learn about how to do things and information to absorb about the world, we are denied many decisions that we are more than capable of making. Too often, we are treated as if we are stupid, because information is wrongly equated with intelligence. I was ridiculed many times for mispronouncing words, for not knowing the answers to Trivial Pursuit questions and for other imagined deficiencies.

The oppression of young people is also enforced by our legal system. Young people are not permitted to vote until the age of eighteen. Yet this age is arbitrary. Why eighteen, and not sixteen? The result is that young people often work, pay tax, and contribute enormously to society but are disenfranchised. Again, arguments that young people are not capable of making a voting decision are based on assumptions about information and intelligence. But many people over eighteen who know very little about our political system or the candidates are required to vote, while well-informed young people are denied this right. Our actual age does not necessarily have a bearing on our social, intellectual or emotional age.

This legal enforcement of the oppression of young people is evidenced in another way. In certain circumstances, it is legal to strike a child, although it would be a criminal offence to do the same to an adult. This treatment is justified in much the same way as striking women used to be. Violence against women by their husbands was permitted for "disciplinary" purposes under the common law as recently as last century. Most Australians would remember the review of a South Australian court judgment in 1993 in which it was stated that it is permissible for a husband to use "rougher than usual handling" to compel his wife to have sex.

Generally, age oppression operates in a similar way to sexism and racism, with young people simply not taken as seriously as older people. They are interrupted, and ignored. For example, in Beijing in 1995, young women were highly visible at the Non-Government Organisations (NGO) Forum but less so at the parallel UN's Fourth World Conference on Women, attended by government representatives. I attended both events as WEL's representative, and at the NGO's caucusing meetings I saw young women acting as couriers for their older counterparts. They were asked to run and fetch and carry, and so missed proceedings. Conscious of what was happening, I refused to run other people's errands, when asked.

I find this kind of disrespect – especially when perpetrated in an environment such as the Beijing conference – to be rather frustrating, because young people have often been at the forefront of political action and movements. For centuries, student activists have put reformist issues on the political agenda, testifying to the intellect and power of young people. Witness South Africa during the struggles against the apartheid regime, China in 1989, the Western world during the 1960s.

Being oppressed on the basis of youth and treated as less than full citizens has a profound and lasting effect. Because we are shown disrespect, we learn that this treatment is acceptable and normal, that young people are stupid and incapable and that the younger we are the more stupid and incapable we must be. We begin to believe it of ourselves and our peers. Small wonder that we are eager to move forward, and leave those years behind. However, we learn age oppression by living it, and as we get older we ourselves start treating younger people with less respect.

Obviously, age oppression makes alliance-building between younger and older generations difficult. For me, being conscious of the pervasive nature of age oppression has been important in my efforts to build a bridge between the women of diverse ages with whom I have worked. In my feminist activism and at WEL, I have learned that it is possible to overcome the hurdles of age oppression. As a result of my experiences, today I have many respectful and loving relationships with women who are ten, twenty, thirty years older than me. I have learned enormously from these women, just as they have learned from me. My experience tells me that when we get the equation right, when we are respectful of each other, understand each other's struggles, we can build a formidable force for change.

For women, sexism and age oppression combine with particular brutality as both forces operate to separate women from each other. Instead, we should work together, alongside one another, presenting a united front against sexist behaviour and practices. It is, after all, in all our interests.

When I was growing up in the 1970s and 1980s, I was surrounded by images of women as bitchy, calculating and manipulative, or as brainless, incompetent and martyred creatures, valuable only for their appearance. The representation of women in daily news, the dearth of women in public life, and images of women being raped and subjected to violence in books, television and films, all make it is easy to see women as socially, politically, economically and physically inferior to men. My family owned a "funny" book called *How to Live with a Neurotic Wife*, and I was told that Canberra's roads went in confusing circles because they were planned by the wife of Canberra's chief designer. Together, everyday encounters such as these serve to reinforce a potent and convincing view of women as lesser than men.

Thankfully, much in my life contradicted these messages. My mother studied and worked, encouraged me academically, went to WEL meetings, and was a strong and independent woman. Yet it was not enough to drown out the constant messages of women's inferiority. I internalised sexist messages in much the same way as I did the oppressive messages about young people. Although I hope my new daughter will encounter less obvious sexist representation of women in our home than I experienced, I have no doubt that she too will be subjected to, and internalise a view of women as inferior.

As a young woman, I found it difficult to reject the demeaning representations of women related to me by people I loved and trusted. As an adolescent, it's hard to reject these views because they are pervasive. In the end, it is easy to see why we feel women are stupid and untrustworthy. Even today, I frequently have to stop myself from judging other women by their appearance or from assuming that because they have made different choices from mine, they are either stupid or, contradictorily, much more intelligent than I am. Internalising sexism makes it very difficult for us to respect each other, value our different thinking and therefore work together. It makes women's organisations amongst some of the toughest places to work! I don't think that any one group is to blame for internalising these messages, but I do think it is within our power to overcome this conditioning. Indeed, we must if we are to have better relationships with all the women in our lives and an effective Women's Movement.

As women get older, the combined force of sexism and age oppression manifests itself somewhat differently. Older people are expected not to play and have fun, nor to have young friends, try new things and experiment in the way that younger people do. Although only in my early thirties I would find it difficult to make a career change, even though it is something that I might enjoy. Likewise, older women are restricted in how they dress and behave. We expect "dignity" and "seemliness", and scorn those who do not recognise their age with derisive judgments such as "mutton dressed up as lamb".

As girls and young women, we are often told that we can't do things we want to. It is too dirty, too difficult, too strenuous, too idealistic, not becoming. Challenging stereo-types and moving beyond these internalised messages can be very frightening. Yet to have the kind of lives we want women of all ages – young and old – must challenge these perceived limits and we must feel the terror.

When I applied for the position of WEL's National Coordinator, it seemed like an outrageous and impossible thing to do. I was twenty-nine, but took over from a woman who had held the position for four years, and had previously been a senior government bureaucrat and worked in the Women's Movement for many years. She was thirty years older than me. If I had believed my feelings, I never would have applied for the job and would have never had gained the experience lobbying, organising and managing.

During my term as Coordinator, I spent a great deal of time feeling terrified. In part, my terror arose because I was challenging a stereotype. As WEL's National Coordinator, I was expected to maintain a high public profile, and represent the organisation to government and the public. I felt as though I carried responsibility for all WEL, and years of socialisation made me doubt whether I was up to the task, even when I knew that I was ready for the challenge.

Our success as women, having the choice to do what we want, when we want and how we want, requires us to move beyond the obstacles of oppression. In my view, we must reclaim our connection with each other, across generations. This requires that we talk together to understand our differences, value our diversity and follow through by supporting each other, celebrating each other, taking delight in each other's successes.

The marginalisation and disenfranchisement of young people breaks the link between older and younger women. Age oppression causes us to criticise and attack each other, often unjustifiably. But young women deserve the respect of older women, just as older women deserve our respect. With knowledge about older women's achievements and experiences, young women today do many things differently from older women, whether this be how we conduct our relationships or simply spend our money. But when faced with prejudice and discrimination, the fastest way to learn is from our friends. We overcome fears and phobias by getting to know the those from backgrounds different from our own. A diversity of friends will enrich our lives at the same time as making us an unstoppable force for change. Together, we can be bold, laugh at our fear, and build alliances across the ages, because young women and older women are perfect allies. We belong together. We may do things differently, but there is room for all of us in feminism.

Lines of Women

Virginia McLean

I am Virginia and I am seventeen years-old. I am becoming a woman, but I am not yet ready to call myself a woman.

I have spent the last fourteen years of my life in a metropolitan private Anglican girls' school. I cannot help but feel naive, girlish. I know that my life is about to change immeasurably, because I will soon leave this institution. I have begun to make increasingly important decisions which will influence my future direction. I watch as my girlfriends enter this same stage, and I see our identity as cheerful, young schoolgirls dressed in blue and white fast slipping away.

As I search for figures with whom to identify, I consider Simone de Beauvoir's major theme in *The Second Sex* (1971), that woman is made, not born. De Beauvoir explored how the course of one's childhood and personal history defines a woman. I reflect upon how my own circumstances have shaped my character. Amongst the yellowing pages of my family's memories, I see the face of a woman in my past. I stop flipping through scenes from my childhood pasted into plastic albums when I come to a photograph taken long before I can remember anything. Below it, I notice a caption written by my (then) five-year-old sister, Heather: "Mummy says this photo is very special because it shows three generations of women (March, 1980)". The photograph is of my mother's mother, my mother, my sister, and me only two-weeks-old. My grandmother, mother and sister squint into the sun. I am lying in my mother's arms asleep, unaware. Today, the photograph has taken on a new significance. No longer is it simply a cute baby shot, just another happy memory in our family history. I begin to realise how little I know about these people who are so important in my life. I want to find out more.

I sit at the kitchen table and ask my mother for the first time about my grandmother. I met her just three times in my life. I want to know what she was like, what choices she made in her lifetime, what things shaped her. My mother tells me stories I have never heard before, stories which I was too young to hear as a child. I learn that my grandmother, Bertine, was amongst the first American women who chose, and was able to stay in employment after World War II, rather than return home to look after a family. During the war, she filled a man's position in a factory which manufactured aeronautical parts. My grandmother always valued the independence that working brought her, and she stayed on in the factory for most of her life. Her choice was not so common in small town America in the 1940s, says my mother. I feel proud of Bertine as I discover her great contribution to history: she helped to manufacture the aeronautical parts that were used in the first spacecraft to land on the moon.

Our conversation turns to my mother's life. I ask her about the choices she made when she was my age. At seventeen, my mother was told that my grandfather did not have any money to invest in her education, and that instead it would go to her brother. My grandfather's presumption was that his money would go to waste if spent on my mother because she would quickly marry, have children and forget her career. Nevertheless, my mother was determined to succeed, even if without training at an expensive university. She began a promising career in publishing in New York City and, when she arrived in Australia, she wrote a nutrition book called *Good Food for Babies and Toddlers* (McLean: 1979).

Since I was born, my mother has spent the seventeen years *at home*. I wonder how she could do this. She was such an active feminist in the 1970s. I am disappointed, even saddened that my mother's feminist stance did not last through the 1980s. However, as we continue to talk, I find that for many years, I have misinterpreted my mother's choice to stay at home. I have confused it with the 1990s' idea that it is unacceptable to be a mother-at-home, and that a woman must work to liberate herself. I come to understand that her decision was not weakness, nor was it conformity. My grandmother was proud of her work, and so is my mother, only hers is of a different nature.

And now, my sister Heather and I are to continue this pattern of liberated women, pursuing their own paths. My sister is already five years down her chosen path, and this has led her to Canberra. I speak to Heather on the telephone and hear the voice of a determined, mature young woman. She discusses the important choices she has already made: she has completed one degree, she has spent a year working in Paris and is currently doing her Masters in development policy. I see my sister as a passionate, capable young woman, with great ambitions for her future. Over the telephone, she says, "I just remember that we were brought up to believe that feminism is very important in our lives". Heather believes that she cannot separate her feminism from our mother's. She is inspired by our mother's involvement in the feminist front of the 1970s, and she hopes to be involved in the Women's Movement through her career. Listening to my sister, I feel so young, as though I have so much to learn, as though I am still the baby in the photograph. But at the same time, I know I am not.

Certainly, I am becoming a "young woman", although I am unsure about the meaning of this new identity. I observe that now, being an active young woman requires much effort. Images in Australian society of the liberated 1990s' woman have become entangled with the ever-present ideals of the traditional woman and motherhood. Today, a woman is multi-tasking, multi-talented, multi-functional, multi-dimensional. She is capable and defiant. She is the educated and high-flying, power-wielding executive bustling through the Sydney CBD. Yet she remains the nurturing, supportive, great mum who "oughta be congratulated". I baulk at the prospect of filling this multitude of roles in the coming years. I am staggered at the strength and resilience of this complex creature. This ill-defined set of modern and traditional ideals makes the turn-of-this-century woman a confusing and elusive role model. I find it very difficult to identify with her.

In her lecture, *A Room of One's Own*, Virginia Woolf urges her young female scholarly audience to "put on the body" of Shakespeare's fictional sister, and allow her "the opportunity to walk among us in flesh" (1929, p. 117). In 1928, when female intellectual freedom was scarce, this was a daring suggestion. However, to a young female audience such as my friends and I, it would not be so controversial. In my school of young women, we have learned to speak out and to express our views freely, and we are confident that we can achieve our aims and desires. But we do not consciously aspire to change patriarchal traditions in our society, nor do we consciously set out to liberate ourselves.

This may be why my friends and I have begun to see feminism as something that does not directly affect us. It seems distant, almost inapplicable to our lives. After all we already have our freedoms. We have grown up with them, and are not really even aware of our social independence or sexual and intellectual freedoms. Without question, they have always been there for us. Once, in a school debate, I was given the topic, "That modern youth has become conservative". Then, I took the side of the affirmative – and I agreed with the proposition. Still, I think that perhaps my generation is neither as revolutionary as our mothers nor as daring as our grandmothers. But I see this not so much as conservatism, and not antithetical to, our own quiet way of continuing the Feminist Movement.

Recently, I was sitting at a table of ten girls from my year at school and with whom I am not particularly close.

It was the farewell dinner for a mutual friend. Sitting at the table together were an odd assortment of personalities. Our conversation focused around plans for next year. As I listened to the aims of my classmates, I was fascinated by the diverse scope of our interests and I was excited by the possibilities their decisions might bring. One of the girls has chosen to go to England, another wants to train in nursing and work in Latin America, another is unsure, but comfortable with this uncertainty. Amongst my closer friends, I see a possible pilot, an engineer, an artist, a doctor, a dancer, and an opera singer. Others, myself included, are undecided. Sometimes my friends and I forget our good fortune. It is easy to forget that we are so optimistic about our future because we have always been given the means, the support and the encouragement to succeed.

In making these choices for the future, based upon our dreams and desires, we are continuing lines of unique women who once struggled to find themselves in a society which would not allow them freedom. We must honour our mothers, grandmothers and great-grandmothers for their brave challenges to the paths women were expected to follow during centuries of patriarchal rule, because today we enjoy the liberty and self-expression for which they fought.

As my girlfriends and I now grapple for an identity in a chaotic storm of hostility and heated debate, we must re-member the women of our past and their strength. Only then can we begin to appreciate the significance of their accomplishments, and their impact on young women's choices today.

Big *f*, Little *f*

Airlie Bussell

Big *f*. Little *f*. One is a political label; the other is a state of mind, a personal philosophy by which to live. This is case sensitivity at its most biting and arouses sensitive responses, opening veins of discussion which everyone, not only women, needs to consider.

For me, feminism is no longer a Feminist issue. It is a fact of life, ever present, yet not a consideration that actively enters my every thought. Feminism is an integral part of my existence, something that impacts upon life so frequently that it has ceased to warrant a separate classification. Being "young" and feeling incredibly impressionable, my own values and ideals remain in a primitive, formative stage, rife with contradictions – a fact that has been highlighted in writing for this collection. Every time I look at this chapter, I have to make changes because each day I change and, with this, so too the nuances of my understanding and outlook evolve.

Without even intending to be a Feminist, I cannot but hold views that are exactly feminist. It is inevitable. I am a woman. Only recently did I stop attempting to trace the origins of my feminism. In the past I compiled a lengthy list of influences, almost it seems, to try to excuse my beliefs. But now, I see that feminism is inherent. It does not require explanation. It does not even require a point of origin. My feminism was there from the beginning, because I am female. I live my life along feminist lines because I can not think or act beyond these parameters. Because I am a woman, I am feminist. It is that simple, for me, now. But of course, if feminism was that indelible to women there never would have been Feminism and feminism. There would not be the schism between generations of women over loyalties to their sex, or the Movement. I now realise that my former search for the reasons behind my beliefs was not in vain.

My education, my family background and the women who surround me have been the immediate influences. Due to both contrivance and accident, I have grown up in an almost exclusively female environment. The conscious decision to place me in a girls' school for the better part of my education was deliberate in its intention to have me surrounded, supported and encouraged by strong women. At almost the same time, my parents divorced; my father moved to another city and I remained with my mother. This has meant that the usual maternal influence increased almost exponentially. By necessity, as much as choice, my life and ideas have been shaped by my extraordinarily close relationship with my mother. Friends have also held considerable (if unwitting) positions of guidance. These women are perhaps by no means extraordinary, but they achieve in small ways which often go unnoticed.

While my interest in these apparently insignificant, unsung events might seem dispiriting, it is important to assess personal successes against a wider perspective. Babushka, my maternal grandmother, is an exemplary example of under-stated female strength, escaping from Japanese-occupied Manchuria to Australia and there, raising four children and always known for her exceptional kindliness and generosity. My other grandmother, Florence Bussell, is no less impressive; a constant source of wonder and strength, reminding me of how far we have come. She divorced in the post-war flurry and raised my father and aunt alone, with little societal support. By contrast, my generation has grown up in a society which is far more accepting and supportive of women than ever before. But we must be careful not to become blasé about our tentative equality, nor forget how hard previous generations fought for the vote, equal pay and fair representation.

Despite all the influences which have helped to form my feminism, it is exactly that; my own interpretation and vital to my individuality. I am a person who has the capacity to learn, grow, explore and ultimately to advance, and while feminist principles do not colour every decision about how I am going to live my life, I can not look at society as a single sexless entity. I have to make the distinction between women and men because there are differences that change the way women and men live their lives. I am still trying to think of an experience that is not affected by gender.

In the past, Feminism briefly presented itself to me as something to consider "most seriously". I took a Feminist reading to every single issue, situation and experience. For some women, this remains the most satisfying and effective expression of Feminism, and perhaps one day I will return to this.

For the meantime, my feminism is deeply personal; it is intrinsic to the way I live.

Voices:

Mapping the Self

The Book of Revelations

Emily Ballou

What other reason is there for writing than to be a traitor to one's own reign, traitor to one's sex, to one's class, to one's majority GILLES DELEUZE AND CLAIRE PARNET: 1987, P. 44.

A Letter Sent To Australia

This place is one of snow and unfamiliarity.

I sit at the computer, writing letters, looking out onto bare trees and trees covered in snow and trees like my crooked little finger. I am listening to Tracy Chapman. I am drinking tea. If it weren't for the snow, I could be back in my own room with wind blowing through the curtains, you say. But the English Breakfast Tea is Decaffeinated. The milk is Skim. The sugar is Nutra-Sweet. I boiled the water in the microwave because there was no kettle.

I am in America. I sit at the computer drinking watery, grey tea.

I ring an old friend.

"So what are your plans?"

"Don't know. I have no idea."

"Do you think you will go to — like you've always wanted to?"

"I guess. Maybe. I have a job."

"But you hate it."

"Yes. But . . . well you know."

"Yes. Well, that's good."

I pretend that there is bougainvillea on my verandah and you are just an easy phone call away. I pretend that I feel happy spending days in a place where the TV is on all day, whether or not anybody is watching it. I try to sit in the other room reading Spinoza, but soon I am too distracted, I too am drawn into the family room, to hear the confessions of so many TV families: this abused child or this ignored wife or this man stealing five million dollars from the insurance policy of his recently murdered daughter, whom he hadn't contacted in ten years and to whose funeral he didn't even bother to show up. The US justice system will pay him his half, because he is legally her father. I watch ten talk shows a day. We thought Oprah and Donahue were the only two? No, there is Maury Povich and Sally Jesse Raphael and Roseanne . . . For every minute of every day, there is a television program; for every minute of every day, one can participate in a confession, one can clap to show support for emotional soliloquies, one can yell and scream for the TV cameras.

This country terrifies me. If I am shot in a Chuck E. Cheese restaurant before I get back to my beautiful Australia, do not let me be buried here; do not let me go down with this dirt, into this unceasing chaos. Do not. In this place I see a great, irrevocable, national loss; a country that believes books are more threatening to its security than guns.

A Story

Once, I was an American girl. I was seven when I knew I didn't want to get any older. I was eight when I knew the blood between my mother's legs meant she was dying. I was nine when I knew all Communists were Evil. I was ten when I was felt up by a man in a jewellery shop and never said anything about it. I was eleven when I started shaving my legs. I was twelve when I began my ten-year experiment in self-starvation. I was thirteen when my best friend was raped in our after-school classroom. I was fourteen when my mother took me to the Clinique counter to have my colours done. I was fifteen when I got my first perm. I was sixteen when I learned that American history was the history of the universe. I was seventeen when I learned that sex stood for slut and not love. I was eighteen when I fell in love with my best friend Kathy. I was nineteen when I never undressed in front of anybody and had sex in the dark. I was twenty when I decided I needed to be married and have had my first child by the age of twenty-seven. I was twenty-one when my bulimic sister attempted suicide. I was twenty-two when I came to Australia and wondered why I couldn't go shopping at three a.m.

And I was twenty-three when I first masturbated and realised what the word Communism really meant.

A Thought

I came here in a cloud of forgetting, washing away with a smear of blue, all that had gone before. I entered the City, this place of light that reflects the self twice, this night and its harbour, this green Bridge that I knew would take me someplace. Its sky was the universe: anything was possible.

I opened my notebook and began to write. I wrote the Bridge, the night, my forgetting. I wrote the sky, my dislocation, my fears. I wrote my emptiness, my fullness. I wrote the Other who was also myself. I read and wrote for five years while I walked the sky and its reverberations of blue on water, and my memory of this country became a five-year fable about a girl who was not herself, but started to be.

Sometimes when I tell it, it is not even a story, but a photograph through which an interior is articulated.

It is a map, on which I mark all the places of awakening.

It is a notebook, in which what has not yet been understood, is nearly written down.

It is a letter, charting a complicated geography of living.

It is a body, a lived body.

And it is a philosophy, with which I finally learned to speak.

But most of the time, it is my revelations, my epiphanies of displacement.

A Photograph

They are her boots, but you wouldn't know that unless I told you. They are obviously new, so brown, still shining, laces pulled tight until she could only feel their grip around her ankles, and the way they held her feet as she walked the new world. But she is not walking, not now. She is stopped, straddling a river which runs between two large rocks. Her left foot is on the left rock, and her right foot on the right rock, and she is still, and she is balanced, and she is between two places, two countries perhaps. The water is cold and fast and pure and speckled with red and green stones.

She has not stopped because she fears crossing, nor because she is awaiting guidance. Her feet are facing forward and the direction I imagine she will travel is not marked by either rock, but by what moves between them.

What moves there is almost inexplicable, something not yet understood, perhaps unfinished, but there is no question that an answer lies ahead and its speed resembles water which, unlike light, quickly becomes hazardous. It drowns the smallest swimming things and in its persistence hurries even the bones to re-configure themselves.

She cannot swim but what she sees mends her voice into an O of epiphany, if there is such a sound, and brings new, blue jewels to the tip of her tongue where she sucks on their possibilities.

A Philosophy

> *A philosophy is neither a monument nor an affect which is blind to it origins and thus in relation to itself, but an effort to shift thinking from one state to another . . .*
>
> MICHELLE LE DOEUFF: 1991, P. 168.

Once upon a time, I went to Paris on a school exchange and a girl held my hand, articulating for the first time, something crucial: "Now that we are in Paris," she said, "we can hold hands."

The perception of some essential truth appeared to me in the shape of a girl's hand. We skipped along, oblivious to everything. Only later did I attempt to put words to the revelation provided by her hand in mine. Later, I thought about exactly what she had said: "Now that we're in Paris, we can hold hands."

I wasn't sure whether it was the being in Paris part or the holding hands part which made the difference. I hadn't even realised until she said it, that we (does "we" mean she and I, or girls in general?) were not allowed to hold hands outside of Paris. Did she mean that elsewhere, it is not customary for girls to hold hands, in the same way that men shook hands instead of hugging? As far as I knew, I was allowed to hug my friends, although we didn't often hug, only when somebody was going away for a long while. Maybe when they cried. Maybe when they were drunk and falling over. But not every day. So perhaps it was only a cultural difference. We could hold hands the way we could also drink cocoa out of a bowl and eat soft, dark chocolate spread down the length of fresh bread for breakfast.

Or maybe it was something about having a moment outside of the high-school eye, that gaze that kept things safe by keeping this group (and this girl) and that group (and that girl) divided. Maybe it was more about the "we" in that sentence, "we can hold hands", about "she" and "I" being able to come together. To share this moment in Paris together, this cold but sunny first day on the other side of the world. The buzz of being away infecting us with love. Love that needed to grasp, to touch, in order to keep it going.

But what I suspected, was that what she said to me that day had everything to do with holding hands and less to do with being in Paris, either culturally or together, and nothing to do with being from different cliques at school.

The revelation was that until then, holding hands with another girl was something I had never thought of doing. And even at that moment, I hadn't thought of it; she had.

She grabbed my hand. She held it. My hand was only the lucky receiver of her divine and creative brilliance. And they were her words ("we can hold hands") that cracked open the realm of the possible. Until that moment, two girls holding hands had not even existed for me, just as feminist theory did not really exist then. It was there in the world, yet unavailable to me.

Later, when I came to Australia, I found both feminism and girls who held girls' hands.

I did not come here intending to start a war on my psyche. Yet if you asked, I would not call my sexuality simply an experiment that worked, but nor would I have seen it as the inevitable conclusion to some pre-ordained plan called my life.

I initially saw it and still do see it more as a philosophy of sex, a politics of life created out of my new consciousness and my many new freedoms; a previously wordless knowledge which could no longer remain buried or unspoken. Once upon a time, I didn't have the strength to shift my thinking, and it needed a good shove. Because like all philosophies, like feminism, a great transformation of the "mindbody" is required if one is to step outside conventions and think for oneself. Once upon a time, I finally arrived in this space (this country, this way of being), and I was forced to change the assembly of my bones. I no longer had the same body; I was no longer the same girl.

A Body and a Notebook

> There are times in life when the question of knowing if one can think differently than one thinks, and perceive differently than one sees, is absolutely necessary if one is to go on looking and reflecting at all
>
> MICHEL FOUCAULT: 1984, P. 8.

145

She has learned to walk, she has learned to love her body, just a little at first, then much, much more. It was as if the landscape was so strong, so raw, yet so apparently bereft of sustenance that she began to crave sustenance from the most unusual places.

She began to read while she crossed the city, back and forth over the Harbour Bridge, her little red notebook scribbled and dizzy. She experimented with ideas of peripheries and belonging as she charted the journey from suburban Sydney into the heart of the city, its university, its cafes, its dyke night-spots, re-enacting daily her passage between two countries, two worlds. Outside to inside and back again. She remembered Nietzsche's belief that philosophy was best undertaken while walking, or even better, while dancing. In this way, every night she became Nietzschean, then crossed back over the Bridge, alone at five a.m., her head still dancing. Some people murmured that she was becoming rather stupid, walking alone that late into the night.

Yet the more she walked the blue length of the city and its endless sky, the more she nibbled at Words; the more she chewed on ideas and discovered whole worlds of thought. She stopped and scribbled: "discourses and practices . . . construct certain sorts of body . . . how bodies are turned into individuals of various kinds" (Gatens: 1996, p. 67). She watched her legs and loved them, their muscles expanding and reaching with each step for places she had not yet dreamed.

This was her feminism, this was her philosophy, and it began with a muscle, with a forward stride and a sense of awe caused by the new sound inside her: the incessant clamour of ideas. She found that she could not separate what she was learning, the ways she was altering herself, from the walking she did every day. She could not unweave this theoretical awakening from the shape of the trees; nor the strength she finally found in her body from the drug of Words; nor this new freedom which allowed her anything, from the eternal capacity of the thought. Both the freedom and the thought made all things possible. "Truly, I am possessed," she realised, "and it is a beautiful, long-awaited feeling."

A Freedom

And so, I (that is she – the girl I try to step out of and write about, as if a forced absence from myself will allow me to see myself more clearly) forced a gap between what I had been and what I was becoming; a gouge in the sand which I traced and reworked with a long driftwood stick. I felt myself letting that other world slowly slide from my being. Those memories of another life, another person altogether whom I couldn't get back, and did not necessarily want back.

I walked this new world and gave birth to many freedoms.

The freedom to desire.

The freedom to love whom I loved.

The freedom to live alone and pay my own way.

The freedom to be awake and the freedom to understand (they are the same freedom).

The freedom to choose a country and find a place in it.

The freedom to write my own becoming.

Yet every now and then when I shave my legs, I still cannot help but think of Communists.

In Contempt

Cassandra Austin

As a six-year-old child, I stood on the edge of a sandbox where some other young girls were refusing to play with a young boy. I watched as a group of boys marched over to the sandbox and called him a "sissy" for wanting to play with the girls. In tune with this, the girls upped their rejection, also calling him a "sissy". Risking my own alienation I informed both boys and girls that sandboxes were not a girls' domain, and that he did not have to play with the boys if he chose not to. Eventually they left him to play where he wanted.

As a thirteen-year-old child, my siblings and I were required to inform a solicitor about our feelings for our mother and father, as part of a court hearing. We felt as though we were being asked to make a choice between our parents. At the time, we asked the solicitor whether or not we were being tape-recorded – all of us fearful of hurting one or other parent. She assured us we were not. During a break in the discussions she was called from the room, and we, following a cord behind the curtains, discovered a tape recorder. From that moment on, to her utter frustration, we refused to speak another word.

There is enormous pleasure in being able to announce one's opinions and reflect aloud on one's perceptions of the world, whether with the written or spoken voice. In part, it is the joy of expression; creating sounds and making sense of the world. It is also the delight of others listening to you.

Women have fought hard for the right to speak and be heard. Their voices required legitimation as though they had little of value to say. Stereotyping, discrimination and (consequently) low self-esteem are the enemies of our slow battle for articulation. Many women today still struggle to be heard. There are so few women in positions of leadership (political and personal) to provide different models of speaking.

Given this history, I am interested in the gains women have made in "voice". In particular, I am concerned with the voice of silence. I don't mean passive silence, or silence which appears consensual, complicit or afraid. I mean silence that is a consequence of women having been *heard*, and silence that involves listening and actively refraining from commenting by voice. The type of silence I am referring to is vocal, but it requires a degree of sensitivity for someone to hear and to understand its meaning.

My belief in the power of silence will be anathema to many of my fellow feminists. But this is precisely the reason I am interested in exploring it. The difficulty feminists have with silence became most evident to me during a reading of *The First Stone* (Garner: 1995). One of the themes wrestled with throughout the book is the unwillingness of the young women to tell "their side" of the story. Garner wavers between respecting their decision – although she admits not understanding it – and finding them contemptuous because of it. Garner's frustration is predictable and palpable, given our expectation that women will tell their stories. What she neglects to appreciate is that feminism itself made it possible for these young women to choose silence and speak only where and when they would. I want to consider the twin notions of resistance by speech and resistance by silence. And I want to show how Feminism should allow silence to become a power.

While feminism may have developed our understanding of patriarchy and its power as a repressive force, the time is now right to recognise power as a productive force. What I'm proposing is that silence is a power.

In the main, feminists concentrate energies on the politics of intersex relations, yet intrasex relations can be every bit as damaging (and/or wonderful). I believe every theory and movement should be scrutinised internally. I particularly want to concentrate on the way women respond to each other's silence. I have always taken feminism very seriously and in so doing, I have experienced a wealth of benefits. I continue to take feminism seriously by questioning it. However, I am painfully aware that criticism can be used to denigrate rather than construct, especially criticism from "within the ranks". Thus, I make my comments with my ear open to a response.

I am a twenty-eight-year-old woman, and I consider it a core function of feminism to assist women to find their voices. However, we should ask which women? Whose voice? And who is listening? Some suggest that feminism provides a framework for individual women's voices; enabling them to speak collectively where there are issues of commonality and to articulate discretely where they differ. Unlike some other general theories, feminism has never struck me as an attempt to define one voice, one experience or to be one expression. Indeed, the term "feminisms" is common usage. For me, feminism's concern is with giving all women voice and encouraging all voices. However, if we are not listening to each other, who else can we expect to listen? Foremost, women must learn to listen to each other, knowing that this communication may not always involve the spoken or written word.

Looking back at sociological feminist texts from Mary Wollstonecraft's *A Vindication of the Rights of Woman* (1792) to Germaine Greer's *The Female Eunuch* (1970), and more recent fictional work such as Marilyn French's *The Women's Room* (1977) and Alice Walker's *The Color Purple* (1982), each writer explores the process of externalising inner thoughts and emotions. There is great emphasis on the need to speak up and speak out. In particular, there is a need to validate experience through words – written and spoken. Over time, and through all kinds of media, women have learned to articulate notions of patriarchy, explore sexuality and sexual response, discern and distinguish the feminine and the female and discuss the sanctioning of labels like "motherhood", "spinster" and "career women". There was a certain deviance attached to speaking out which made it doubly important for women to find their own voices, as Mary Wollstonecraft wrote:

> *The severest sarcasms have been levelled against the [female] sex, and they have been ridiculed for repeating "a set of phrases learned by rote", when nothing could be more natural, considering the education they receive, and that their "highest praise is to obey, unargued" – the will of man* (1988, p. 259).

The importance of articulating issues has not disappeared, nor has the need to reshape them through naming or redefining lessened. Indeed the second wave of feminism ushered in social and legal enunciation of feminist principles, such as sex discrimination and equal opportunity legislation which was passed in the 1970s and 1980s. Given this, why do I insist on the need to recognise silence?

We find numerous examples of women forced to speak, sometimes against themselves, if we travel back in history. The Salem witch hunts provide a well known example. Women have often been held in contempt of court as a result of their failure to speak. We continue to recognise the power of refraining from speech testified by tools such as the subpeona which is specifically designed to break an individual's silence. Silence has long served as a form of resistance. However, our era's fascination with "media coverage" heightens the importance of recognising and respecting silence.

Within today's more sophisticated modes of power, the media is a main locus for the power of speech. Deliberately (and for obvious reasons), the media promotes speech as the primary power. All forms of media encourage and incite speech acts that produce "cross-fire" – putting opponents face to face. When opposing parties are reluctant to disclose their views, spoiling the media fireworks, there's always someone to step in and provide (alternative) "truths". Society now has more difficulty with the lack of speech than with the act of speech. As Michel Foucault demonstrates "power" is more concerned with producing behaviours than repressing them (1980). This is particularly pertinent in relation to speech acts, where the emphasis is on demanding, manufacturing, and cataloguing the voice. As women, we now have to be careful that our voices are not split, fractured or moulded into forms we cannot recognise. It is easier to manipulate what is said than what is not said. The most vilified comment is now "no comment".

Even as a child I was aware of the importance of negotiating the demands for my speech and my silence. As I stood on the edge of the sandbox, I spoke for someone else who was unable to speak for himself. As the eldest of four siblings asked to provide information that we weren't sure we wanted to provide – especially not after the lie about the tape recorder – I lead us into silence. It is important to recognise that this act of silence in the solicitor's office was no less powerful an act of resistance than the act of speech at the sandbox. Yet this is still difficult for us, as feminists, to understand.

Some years ago, I was raped by a man pretending to be a policeman. After the rape I attempted to act as though nothing had happened. I did not report the crime. I forbad my family to speak to me about it. I continued with my studies and frequented the locale where I was assaulted. Of course this behaviour did not last very long. I was suffering from post-traumatic stress syndrome and eventually I broke down, faced what had happened and how I felt and allowed my family "in".

During this time, a counsellor suggested I report the crime to the police. I did this with grave apprehension – not only because at that stage, I still believed the man was a policeman[1] but also because I was not yet ready to provide nameless people with a clinical account of an "event" that had happened to me.

I am fully aware of the numerous occasions where abused women refuse to speak out about their oppressors and abusers. I am also aware that this makes the oppressors and abusers effective silencers. However, until that point I was unaware of how important it was for me to listen to my internal voices before I faced the questioning, searching, assisting, accusing and public voices of others. I have studied criminology and psychology, and have read widely about the ways in which young women cope with rape – everything from shame through to self-mutilation. This left me in a position of great personal conflict. While I already knew what feminist agencies advised and all about "inappropriate" and "illogical" responses, I could not speak the words nor take the actions "necessary". I needed that silence for myself.

Do not misunderstand me. Along with Wollstonecraft and a host of others, I champion the need to bring to light

---

1 Events later proved that he was using a false badge, and I was only one of a number of women on whom he had used the ruse.

the assaults committed against women and children. I am not suggesting that women should hold these abuses alone, nor keep them from the public eye; I firmly believe there is a measure of responsibility involved. I do not write of my experience in isolation but as a result of six years of employment in the field of criminology. During this time, I have worked as an advocate for homeless people, including women and children from domestic violence backgrounds.

What I have witnessed and what I have felt is simply that there is a definite need for space and silence after an event that somehow changes one's sense of self. I submit that part of knowing how to stand and speak, is first listening to the voice(s) within yourself. And to do this internal listening, we require exterior silence. But neither the silence of others nor the silence expressed by the self is a sign of weakness. It is not a shame. It is not a guilt borne of complicity. It is a strength. This silence paves the way for voice. Unless we recognise this, we feminists wield the harshest and most penetrative weapons against each other as we push each other toward the microphone.

Sexual, physical and emotional violence are not to be tolerated in the home or anywhere else. We should know most abuse involves a male perpetrator, and women and children represent a significant proportion of victims. Women have long acted as advocates for each other and for children, raising their voices against these injustices and seeking atonement and prevention. To achieve these broad objectives, women and men must continue to vocalise their dissatisfactions with the status quo.

Yet, where individual women victims have been reluctant to speak out, to vocalise and name names, it is often feminists who are their fiercest critics. Unwillingness to speak out is often misunderstood by these feminists. Like Garner, they often misinterpret a woman's unwillingness to speak out about a violent home or partner. While we all acknowledge the penalties associated with speaking out (public disbelief, ostracisation, further abuse), silence is frequently taken to suggest (in varying degrees) consent or complicity. But there is no consent in this silence. I draw your attention to the distinction between passive silence – borne of fear – and active silence – the silence of which I speak – which is a necessary requirement for strengthening the self. When we criticise active silence, we are reading what we think we see and hear, not what may be there to see or hear.

In many ways, feminists are supportive of the women who adopt active silence in their personal lives. I have worked with women in domestic violence refuges who are relieved when other women refrain from judging the violence they have experienced, when they are reluctant to speak about it at that point in time. This is especially important, because given time and support, many women *will* speak out.[2] Feminists also recognise that women do not want to trade on "victim experiences", where one group of "victims" is forced to compete against another for political attention, public awareness and resources. The personal may be political, but it also must be allowed to remain personal. Perhaps "being forced to speak" is the converse (and equivalent) to "being silenced".

---

2 But cultural notions of right and wrong seem predicated on the notion that one must rise instantly to correct a wrongdoing – rather than wait and gather resources and strength enough to do so properly and effectively – otherwise guilt is implied. While this may be accurate in some cases, it does not make sense in *all* cases.

There may come a time where women require other women to speak for, or with them, to shatter public silence. This can be done without specificities, allowing effected individuals to focus on making decisions that affect their own lives. Again, this is not about retaining victim status. Rather, it is about recognising and working within complex contexts and focusing on prevention. It is paramount that feminism understand and incorporate the partnership between silence and voice.

There is a complexity here that the above observations perhaps belie. There are also some things that we cannot verbalise; that we can only know. It is not that they are unspeakable, they are just unable to be expressed appropriately or accurately, or forcefully. To attempt to name and describe these things precisely is, in some ways, arrogance. Language, as a vehicle of human rationality and "truth", can only know the limits or edges of some experiences. Yet we ask it to replicate, delineate or capture those experiences for us and for consumption by others. If language can only express its inadequacy, why force it?

Perhaps the young women subjects in Garner's *The First Stone* believed that the words they used to tell their story could not capture their experience, or alternatively that Garner's literary interpretation of their recounted experience would not be "true"[3]. One of the two young women's voices can now be heard under the pseudonym XX in the recent publication *bodyjamming* (Mead: 1997). XX chooses not to relate her version of the events, and instead makes the case against speaking with Garner and the media. While XX

---

3 It is vital to remember that the young women did choose to speak to other individuals and institutions – just not Helen Garner.

justifiably rails against feeling silenced, she states, as others of us know, that the opinion of those close to her is more important than public perception, and that she did not feel as though she could "safely speak" to the media. She notes that:

> This book gives me the possibility of fair representation for the first time. This is the best opportunity I have had to communicate my experience (1997, p. 59).

Yet so often it was assumed that XX and the other young woman were hiding. Insidiously, their silence was used to construct false voices rooted in fear, guilt and hatred. Disappointingly, many of these assertions came from women who call themselves feminists.

When we use silence it is clear that we must be prepared to face public accusations of cowardice or complicity. When contemplating a strategy of silence, we must be certain that our stance is not founded on martyrdom. Yet correcting public perception must be measured against private gain. Even without the piece in *bodyjamming* (surrounded as she was by other women's voices), I suspect it was far more personally valuable and powerful for XX to withhold the words, rather than to lose them by making them available for general perusal and dissection. To my mind, by the very act of refusing to speak to Garner, the young women revealed a sophisticated understanding of the power of silence. They anticipated the use of their lived experience as media fodder – we have to consider our audience when we decide (not) to speak.

And where do we learn this strength, if not from feminism? I know that with the help of silence, it is possible to see the essence of things. We need silence *in* speech to organise, emphasise and counterbalance the spoken. This is not to say that verbalising our thoughts or experiences is unnecessary; just that in practice we need to be open to difference, and this includes difference in language, expression and indeed the need to articulate. For me understanding this is true wisdom.

I wanted to create a dialogue about the importance of conscious silence. I hope I have demonstrated why silence is not always a disempowering choice for women. It is paradoxical that feminism has granted us the power of silence – something that women have worked so hard to overcome. Yet closer examination allows us to see that the *choice* to be silent does not fit the accepted "wisdoms". I see that we have so needed to hear and celebrate our own voices that we continue to characterise our silences as "negative" or absent. Silence has a history, a form, a presence, and I know that it is a necessary component of voice.

In this third wave of feminism, we need to embrace the power of silence. Silence has new meaning because it has become a legitimate choice, rather than a forced passivity. This is not an internal backlash against earlier needs. This is an ability won only through verbalisation, to make the decision not to speak. Now, we must listen carefully, to hear the silence.

I don't miss the irony of exploring the relevance of silence through the written and spoken word. I must write and speak if I am to reach a general audience. Yet this is not where success lies because in the general, a simplification is often born. Instead, it is the individual examples where silence and/or speech can empower us that are crucial.

Scattered Speculations on Being a White Feminist

Krysti Guest

> [I]t may be pointed out that whereas Lehman Brothers, thanks to computers, "earned about $2 million . . . for 15 minutes of work", the entire economic text could not be what it is if it could not write itself as a palimpsest upon another text where a woman in Sri Lanka has to work 2,287 minutes to buy a t-shirt. The "post-modern" and the "pre-modern" are inscribed together
>
> GAYATRI CHAKRAVORTY SPIVAK: 1988, P. 171.

This decidedly un-sassy and difficult quote is probably not the brightest way to begin an account of my passionate relationship to feminism. It would, no doubt, be far more seductive to skate in with a hip-chick-rave and at least flash a bit of street cred up-front, rather than trudging onto the page with indecipherable words like "palimpsest" (a parchment on which the writing has been partially removed to make room for new writing). This quote could send you to sleep or at least invoke a bristly resistance to what is setting itself up as a serious, intellectual rant.

But as un-hip, hardline or scary-humourless-feminist as it might seem, I am a little weary of "young feminists" being represented as only worded up on groove culture, cyberpunk and lipstick, resistant to the joyless politics caught up in the term "feminist". Because, *hello*, there are one or two things in the world which are pretty damn joyless, which are complex to understand and which oppress women. Figuring out why the majority of the world's refugees are women is not my idea of fun but it is partly my idea of being a feminist. So, I have kept the quote because it has fundamentally affected my understanding of my identity as a white, Australian feminist, and I hope it will be understood as a way of framing the following snapshots of what feminism means to me.

Travelling From the Known

When I was twenty, I believed that as a *person*, I was naturally capable of doing anything I attempted. Consequently, I saved $4000 of waitressing pay, deferred study, packed my backpack and travelled throughout Europe and South and Central America for more than two years. In Europe, my self-identification as a person was persistently fractured by an endless stream of sexual harassment, designed to mark me as a woman, and hence, not permitted to freely take up public space. However, this ever-present gendered encroachment on my sense of freedom was not significantly disabling: I was far more fascinated with my increasingly robust survival skills. With my belief in individualised self-preservation blossoming, I traipsed off to South America with very long, bright blonde hair, all the wrong shoes and no inoculations. But most importantly, I had no understanding of South America's long history as a site for European colonisation and exploitation and with no such interpretative political framework, the extreme poverty and deprivation which I witnessed was as incomprehensible as it was distressing.

However, at least one experience wrenched me from a general benevolent pity for the people around me to nascent politicisation. On the border of Bolivia and Peru lies Lake Titicaca, which in traveller/tourist circles is famous for its floating islands made out of reeds, growing through the Lake's surface. I took a tourist boat to one of the tiny islands, and as I was wandering around I realised that we were marching on the "front gardens" of these people's houses, stepping over the fish they were drying in the sun for their dinner. We manoeuvred around Uro Indian women wearing the historically enforced, colonial dress of bowler hats, weaving bracelets for us to buy and avoiding my gaze. A group of children greeted the boat and screamed "Give us money", in five different languages. Some American tourists decided to give out some sweets. There were not enough lollies for all the children and when we left, some remained at the island's shore screaming.

After we finished trampling all over these people's lives and boated back to the mainland, I was overwhelmed with a sense of shame. I understood hazily for the first time that my travelling was not innocent, that my Western freedoms were predicated on enforcing a lifestyle of bracelet weaving, desperate children and the selling of privacy. And that somehow in amongst this entangled story of freedom and oppression, I was as responsible for branding the Uro women with those bowler hats, the signs of European culture, as were the Spanish colonialists.

When I returned to Australia it was 1988, the bicentenary

of European colonisation and indigenous dispossession and the year that the Labor Government introduced a graduate tax and a policy of aligning tertiary education directly with business needs rather than critical scholarship. These politically charged events converged with an inarticulate sense of outrage at the injustice I had witnessed in the world, with my experience of relentless sexual harassment and a profound disbelief that my education had never included any analysis whatsoever of such issues. I discarded my naive beliefs that individuals control their own destiny and that we could all be free and equal if only we tried hard enough. I began studying Marxist, feminist and anarchist political theory and I threw myself into community-based political activism.

Situating Responsibility

Feminism is a floating, butterfly word, the meaning of which can ostensibly be captured with the utmost simplicity (stopping the oppression of women) but which also flits in complex and fractal ways.

To me, feminism is not a finite thing, an accessory to parade in certain social situations and hide during dinner to avoid any unpleasantness. Feminism is a process; a way of thinking about the world, about knowledge, about power, about politics, economics and identity. It is a kaleidoscope through which to view and understand the injustice, violence, oppression and exploitation of the world from the perspectives of women – perspectives which consequently offer possibilities to create freedom and justice for all women. At the same time as this public political analysis, feminism to me is a passionately embodied, personal ethic.

It filters how I understand myself and shapes how I desire to be in the world. It offers a chain of revelations about how I take up space in my community, and the impact of that space on the liberty of others.

As with all conceptual frameworks, particular notions of feminism are limited by the specific values of the community from which they arise. Looking at feminism as both emancipatory and limited, it is interesting to tease out some current interpretations of the popular feminist concept of "speaking personally". To speak personally has been a key strategy by which feminists have reworked experiences – previously dismissed as "merely personal"– into sites of public, political struggle. However, in the dominant voice of Western feminism, an almost ritualistic commitment to the mode of an individualist confession has recently destabilised the political foundations of "speaking personally". This mode of "speaking personally" translates the catchcry "the personal is political" into "only the personal is political, or worse, "only the personal is remotely interesting". Accordingly, politics or collective action fade in favour of fiercely disorganised personal choices.

It would be easy to see claims that feminism is now "largely about individual practice and taking on personal challenges" (Bail: 1996, p. 16) as merely part of a fashionable, cult of the individual world view. However, it seems to me that the celebration of this view partly arises from confusing the notion of individual preference with the thorny question of determining *difference* between women.

For decades, different groups of indigenous women, third-world women, working-class women, lesbian women, women with disabilities have loudly pointed out that the political analysis and strategies generated by white, Western feminists often falsely universalise white women's experiences. By failing to engage with racial, social, economic and other structural differences between women, this brand of dominant feminism remains either irrelevant or oppressive to the majority of the world's women as it can not come to terms with the specificity of different groups of women's oppression.

These questions of "differences" within feminisms are of fundamental importance. However, responding to their demands for recognition of difference by bunkering down under individualist confession that *only* focuses on personal preferences and different experiences, fundamentally misses the point. The relevant "differences" between women are not personalised preferences nor are they naturally occurring attributes. More significantly, they are differences generated through social, political and economic networks of power. The fact that women corporate lawyers get paid about eight times the amount that rape crisis workers do is not because corporate law is naturally more valuable than rape crisis work. The difference is generated from the fact that our "free market" economy values big business significantly more than it does stopping violence against women. Indigenous women are not subject to police harassment on a far greater scale than white women because they are naturally more criminal, but because of systemic racist prejudices within the Australian justice system.

Smothering these *systemic* questions of difference under a constant chatter of individual approaches ends up allowing some pretty nasty systems of oppression to remain invisible, and invisibility breeds power. This is precisely the problem with *only* focusing on individual practice and personal challenges: it snaps the connection between individual experience and the fact that such experiences are, to a significant degree, determined by one's gender, class, racial background. As that connection snaps, so too does the ability to devise solutions to the foundations of the various forms of women's oppression.

That snap also allows us to remain blind to the way in which our society currently generates differences which not only allow particular groups of women (white, first-world, usually middle-class) greater access to certain equalities and freedoms, but keep us oblivious to the fact that such access and benefit is, in highly complex ways, contingent on the social and economic oppression of other groups of women elsewhere in the world. As a white, Australian woman, I have become committed to understanding the slippery and complicated issues which permit me, as a white Australian woman, to benefit from the oppression of different groups of women. I hazily understood this idea when the strong foreign exchange rate allowed me to trample over the lives of the women of the Peruvian floating islands on Lake Titicaca. It is the freezing realisation that my relative sense of cultural and psychological stability as an Australian is founded on a black history of stolen children, genocide and dispossession, a history which is still continuing as indigenous communities defend their native title against racist government agendas and our Prime Minister hollers in contempt at Australia's first Reconciliation Convention.

Generating responses to these issues has absolutely nothing to do with emblazoning guilt on anyone's forehead or dredging up the patronising charity mentality whereby the relatively privileged help to save the poor-unfortunate-types. On the contrary, linking questions of systemic benefit to systems that produce "difference" as oppression allows us to begin *taking responsibility* for the implications of our nationally, and internationally, interconnected societies. Its focus on interconnections entails, at least, rubbing acid on those complacent stories we tell ourselves about our communities, in an attempt to decipher the lines of invisible ink. As with a palimpset, it is these hidden stories that glue our social systems together.

Tracing Global Stories

In 1995, I once again packed my backpack, this time to attend the Non Government Organisation (NGO) Forum on Women in Beijing. With over 35 000 participants, it was the largest gathering of women in the history of the world. For me, surrounded by women from all over the globe, passionately detailing their experiences of oppression and fiercely debating how best to fight for freedom and justice in their communities, the Forum was intoxicating. I had tangible confirmation of global solidarity between women.

However, far greater than this sense of connection, was my profound sense of disconnection from the dominant issues. I heard, repeated like a mantra from many feminist networks in developing countries and a few from developed countries, that the critical issues which feminists must urgently address were the increasing globalisation of the capitalist economy, the unbridled power of multinational corporations and the recolonising effects of international financial and trade institutions. As these issues rarely circulate within feminist discourse in Australia, it is useful to outline them briefly before considering how they have shifted my experience as a white feminist.

The glossy phrase "economic globalisation" generally refers to the current, unprecedented expansion of multinational capitalism throughout the world; the free market ethos no longer fettered by State socialist blockage. The forces behind, and benificiaries of, this increasing economic integration are Western-based, multi-national corporations, which operate primarily within the industries of agriculture, pharmaceuticals, arms, mining and increasingly services and telecommunications. These corporations wield immense and highly concentrated political and economic power, controlling over thirty-three per cent of private global assets, seventy per cent of international trade, and generating sales of over seven-trillion dollars each year in international trade. Their exponential blossoming can be linked to the strict deregulation and privatisation policies of the International Monetary Fund, the World Bank and international trade agreements.

The detrimental effects of globalisation on an individual country's economic, social and cultural rights have been savage, deepening the level of world poverty and entrenching inequality between the First and Third worlds. Through economic might, geographic flexibility and subcontracting, the employment offered by such corporations is often precarious and dangerous, taking place under abusive conditions.[1]

Some of the most garish of these working conditions involve deliberate abuses of women's human rights. For example, in the factories of Economic Processing Zones (designated areas in many developing countries designed to lure multinational investment through subsidised infrastructures, tax

---

1   For an introductory discussion of the effects of this form of economic globalisation on the enjoyment of human rights see: Susan George (1988); Anne Orford (1997); Vandana Shiva (1997).

incentives and the promise of non-unionised working conditions), the workforce is primarily made up of unmarried women aged between eighteen and twenty-five and child labour is increasing. Working conditions are primitive and any resistance is met with sacking, and in many cases physical and sexual violence. These primitive conditions are also flourishing in Western countries. An Australian Senate Committee inquiry has identified that there are between 50 000 and 330 000 clothing and textile "outworkers" in Australia.[2] Trapped in an informal sector, these primarily migrant and refugee women often work eighteen-hour days for as little as fifty cents to two dollars an hour, and are subjected to non payment, unreimbursed expenses and physical and verbal harassment.

Other spectacles of gendered oppression, fuelled by economic globalisation were named at Beijing. The poverty, inequality and economic networks bolstered by globalisation can be linked to the growth of multinational trafficking in women and children from countries such as Nepal, India, Bangladesh, Burma, the Philippines and Thailand. Similarly, in countries such as the Philippines and Thailand, sex tourism increased exponentially when their governments and the International Monetary Fund identified tourism as a strategy for servicing foreign debt.

At a political level, government control over hitherto public arenas such as industrial policy, health schemes, and education policy has been severely curtailed, if not abolished through the imposition of "structural adjustment programs" in many countries. As one commentator has

---

2 Senate Economics References Committee: *Outworkers in the Garment Industry*. December 1996.

argued, such shifts are creating a "new international political order, whereby the recently won sovereignty of Third World nations has been substantially eroded" (Stamp: 1994, p. 12). A new era of colonisation.

Switching Lenses

As someone who generally thought of herself as pretty up on cutting-edge feminist issues, listening to these insistent, eloquent and highly sophisticated analyses of the global economic web and its impact on women's human rights was a humbling experience. I was ashamed and appalled that in my educated and activist life I had never encountered these issues before. I again realised that what we think of as "knowledge" is always limited and often deceptively safe. The official Government Fourth World Conference on Women's Platform for Action also fails to address any of these global economic concerns. And it seems to me that the reason why these global economic issues do not circulate within certain Australian feminist discussions or government-sanctioned agendas is that they are the invisible ink stories of our Western communities which are necessary to glue together our more visible narratives about individual freedoms, democracy and justice. Like a palimpsest, post-modern and pre-modern social conditions were inscribed together in the stories of the women at Beijing.

My experiences at Beijing dramatically redirected my personal and professional life. Although I was already employed as a women's rights adviser, I reconstellated my focus and began studying and organising around the effects of economic globalisation and international trade

law on human rights both within Australia and internationally. I placed myself in a position to be able to unravel
and make visible the interconnected post-modern and pre-
modern conditions so powerfully articulated at the Forum.
It seemed a responsible way to engage with the insistent
demands of the Forum's women for economic and social
justice and a way to take responsibility for my privileged
position in the debate.

Making a commitment to highlight these issues and to
devise strategies which run interference with oppressive
global economic systems has led me in two connected
directions. Firstly, I recognised that globalisation is not
something occurring "out there" in that other world inhabited
by starving Somalis, rather it is entwined in Australia's social
and political economy. This understanding shifts the
boundaries of political struggles and demands. Australia's
increasing malleability to multinational corporate power is
illustrated by the constant chatter about tariff reduction
and the commitment to privatise what were once our "public"
utilities. Most significantly, the Australian government is
directly implicated in facilitating the safe passage of multinational mining on Australian indigenous people's lands,
on Bougainville and in East Timor, where the struggles for
self-determination are oppressively denied on the basis of
mineral and oil resources.

But, immensely more difficult for me than merely sign-
posting the oppressive aspects of globalisation, is trying to
trace how a majority of people in Australia, including a
majority of women, benefit as a group from the oppressive
dynamics of our current global economy. This requires
coming to terms with some basic mechanics of international capitalist economics. It means, for example, asking

why a set of saucepans from an Indonesian factory are relatively "cheap" – certainly cheaper than a set made in Australia – and therefore attractive to Australian consumers. No one's labour is inherently cheap. The value of labour is the product of political and social struggles. Maintaining pools of cheap labour in developing countries is critical for corporate – and shareholder – profit.

Considering economic value in this way up-ends assumptions that developing countries are the First World's rather backward cousin, who we try benevolently to feed through rock concerts and hand-outs. Conversely, the poverty of these nations is essential for the First World's corporations gain and their consumers' access to cheap goods. The developing world becomes the invisible framework which supports the developed world's economic (and by implication political and social) power basis. A palimpsest is created so that the stories of the wretchedness and poverty of the majority of the world are hidden from view to make room for capitalist emancipatory narratives of consumerist freedom of choice and democratic superiority.

Asking these questions about the hidden and oppressive systems that underpin my relatively privileged life is primarily what it means to me to be a white Australian feminist right now. It is a way of constructing some framework for a possible political engagement with the women at the Forum and with the women of Lake Titicaca. It is one strategy with which I can attempt to overcome the most repellent aspects of the benevolent colonialist approach of a white, Western feminism which sees all women's oppression as the same and consequently forecloses the possibility of political strategies which respond to specific forms of other women's oppression. And it is a way of conceptualising the differences between women with a vibrancy that is personally confronting and politically meaningful – the dual movement of feminism's demand "the personal is political". As Chandre Talpade Mohanty so wryly commented almost two decades ago:

> *[S]isterhood cannot be assumed on the basis of gender; it must be forged in concrete, historical and political practice and analysis* (1984, p. 339).

Seeking a Place[*]

Stephanie Gilbert

In this discussion, I want to talk about some of the issues and thoughts I have had during the current debates about land rights (Native title, Mabo and Wik)[1] and the stolen generation, particularly in the media. I want to leave you

---

* A slightly different version of this chapter was first given at the 6th Women and Labour Conference; Deakin University, 29 November–1 December 1998.

1 Debates in Australia about Aboriginal and Torres Strait Islander land rights have intensified during recent years as a result of the landmark Mabo and Wik judgments on the legal fiction of *terra nullius*, loosely, "land belonging to no-one". Native title is the term used in legislation passed by the Commonwealth Government to deal with the outcomes of the Mabo and Wik judgements.

with two points by the end of this chapter. The first is that patriarchy doesn't play favourites with any women. Thus, issues affecting Aboriginal communities must also be understood within a patriarchal framework. Secondly, we must recognise and commit to the ideal that the personal is political.

At present, we are living in an Australia where the words Mabo, Wik, Native Title and Stolen Children are bandied around in public rhetoric with little apparent understanding of what they actually mean. As an Aboriginal woman, I have a real commitment to seeing each of these issues worked through, so that Aboriginal people finally are credited with what is rightfully ours. At the same time, however, I sometimes feel very distant from these debates, and that's a conflict that I'm struggling with. Why the conflict? Well, while on the one hand, I understand much of the intricacies of Wik and Mabo and the native title debate, on the other hand, we are talking about issues that are real for some Aboriginal people and not for others.

Overwhelmingly, I feel that these debates don't really involve me. Over the past three years, there has been a real shift of focus away from the social devastation which remains in our communities to land issues. What appears to have happened is that there has been a movement away from what could loosely be termed "women's business" – the issues which involve social conditions – and one towards "men's business" – mining, land, capital investment and the economy. When we look at the debates on television, apart from Lois O'Donohue, we don't see many Aboriginal women. Torres Strait Islander people are even rarer. We see men like Noel Pearson and others paraded across the screen. These men are presented explaining the intricacies of legislation or land claims, explaining the position of their constituents.

I am concerned about the implication of this whole focus on land, as if our relationship with the land excludes other things. It seems to be a continuation of a divide-and-rule tactic. If we focus on land, then we only include those people involved in that pursuit. It forces people to align with one group of people and not others. It may create distinctions between people that may not have existed before. As Aboriginal people, we don't concentrate on our collective good because the systems we're given create division. What seems to be occurring is the continuation of the colonisation project. We, as Aboriginal people, are being divided once again. Previously it was overt. We were divided on the basis of our biological inheritance. Now it seems to be not only about our biology, but also includes our enculturation.

Native title is only directly relevant to some people. To be eligible to claim land, you must be able to show an ongoing ownership, custodianship or use of land. Well, if your land was stolen, or if you were, your chances aren't great. So, what we have is a denial of all those Aboriginal people who don't fit the categories for native title eligibility. Once again, the "real Aborigine" versus the "not-quite-so-real Aborigine" scenario is showing its ugly head. Of course, I have to be nervous about that.

I had hoped when the report of the Inquiry into the Removal of Aboriginal and Torres Strait Islander Children[2] came down on 26 May 1997, that it would present an opportunity for change, but the power of patriarchy put an

---

2   In 1995, the then Commonwealth Attorney-General asked the Human Rights and Equal Opportunity Commission to hold this inquiry, after social action by Aboriginal organisations.

end to that. What I forgot was that children are "women's business". I forgot that if men had decided that it was all right to take children, there was no way they would now apologise without "good reason". Overwhelmingly, our experience of the Inquiry has been that the men involved have done the legal work, the administrative work, the media presentation of the document and calls for legislation and reaction from governments, the "hard work". And what we don't see in the media – but Aboriginal people see it behind the scenes – is the women picking up the mess that has been left by another inquiry into another part of our lives. So the "second stealing" has taken place by the men in charge, again. For those people whose lives the inquiry was investigating, this is the second stealing of their lives; my life. Previously, our lives were stolen to be improved. Now they are stolen for public display. We became the new topic of discussion, and our lives are the tissues people wiped away their tears with when they heard our stories. The pain of the second removal has had little recognition, our pain seemingly has no place in the high-powered discussions of right or wrong.

Even reconciliation has been co-opted for the native title debate. Reconciliation has at its heart, land rights for Aboriginal and Torres Strait Islanders, but it also involves many other issues. There are a whole lot of people in the communities that I live in who don't relate to the concept that land is life. No one is talking about the fact that nowadays spending on health is less per head for Aboriginal people than non-Aboriginal people. I think that in our move towards the future, we have to find some way to make peace with both groups of issues.

It is really wonderful to see over the past months, people turning much more their personal beliefs into public action

– social and political action. In many ways, it is quite stimulating and affirming to see people involved where they haven't been before. A lot of the movement forward that Aborigines have done over the period of colonisation has occurred with the assistance of people from outside Aboriginal communities, and I don't think that that should stop.

In our commitment to social change, we need to think about a couple of things. The first thing that we need to think about are the processes of colonisation of this land. The fact that there was the taking of land, there was the stealing of children. We need to get to a stage where instead of just interacting with this knowledge at an intellectual level, we bring it to a personal level, because people talk about it as if it exists "out there" when it doesn't.

We need to look at what has happened, and what the issues are, and think about our reactions and our feelings. The next question which people need to ask themselves, one which I think has become a bit lost, is: "Do you believe in self-determination for Aboriginal people as Aboriginal people define it?" And you need to answer; not just ask the question of yourself, but actually answer it. The level of analysis that Aboriginal people are forced to be involved in is much more than just watching the news on television. So it seems fair that all Australians do the same level of analysis and musing.

But in the debate about native title, I hope self-determination has not become the sacrificial lamb. Ultimately, the question is whether or not you actually believe in the assimilation of Aboriginal and Torres Strait Islander people – one Australia which allows for no difference. If you don't, then what are you going to do about it? I don't think we've buried the assimilation project yet. '

Australians have moved forward in their relationships with Aborigines by working together, and that should not stop. Reconciliation requires the involvement of us all. Not just sighing praises in the living room, but putting pen to paper, sometimes foot to pavement. Being active, but not appropriating Aboriginal culture. This needs to happen because Aboriginals are under fire from every angle. Our culture is being appropriated, our access to justice seems also to be disappearing.

The complacency must end because patriarchy hasn't ended and just as Aborigines are under attack, so are women. Patriarchy has been one of the tools used to divide us, but we don't have to endure this alone. After all, we are you. We are an essential element of Australia. It is not possible to live in Australia without experiencing our presence in some way. So for all of us, the personal must be political. Just as my life became a political football, so might yours. Our obligation is to each other, as women, Aborigines, Australians, humans.

Acting Up

Lines of Demarcation: Beijing 1995

Suzette Mitchell

We represent more than half of the world's population, but our voices are rarely heard in the halls of power. War, violence and environmental degradation leave a legacy of destruction for future generations. If we are to inherit these and other problems, then we want to share responsibility now for their solutions. Therefore, we must be allowed to participate actively and effectively at all levels of decision making
UNITED NATIONS FOURTH WORLD CONFERENCE
ON WOMEN: YOUTH DECLARATION.

For me, as a young Australian feminist, nothing has been as intellectually, emotionally, or logistically exciting as my involvement in the preparations and staging of the United Nations (UN) Fourth World Conference on Women in Beijing and associated Non-Government Organisation (NGO) Forum in the (not so) nearby town of Huairou, in 1995.

The Beijing Women's Conference stands as illustration that the much-hyped "generational debate" is largely mythical, constructed by the media to give good copy. As I saw it, Australian women worked together towards Beijing, unconcerned about age, ethnic background, sexual preference, religion and economic status. Indeed, the whole process revealed that young Australian feminists sometimes have more in common with older Australian women, than with our youthful feminist colleagues overseas. Nevertheless, the knowledge and wisdom we gained from working alongside motivated and intelligent young, feminist women from around the world, has strengthened the international perspectives of young Australian feminists.

I was a member of the Australian Council for Women (ACW), which was established to advise and assist the Australian government with its preparations for the Beijing conference. As a member of the Council, I repres- ented Australia in Beijing, and I was also a member of the official delegation to the regional UN Conference on Women, held in Jakarta in 1994. At this meeting, I was the only young woman in any of the government delegations.

Internationally, "youth" is defined as the time after child- hood and before adulthood – between eighteen and thirty – so I scrape in by the skin of my teeth. Theoretically, this is when "youth" learn how to be responsible adult citizens. In practice, it means something very different in the West or the "North" and the developing world or the "South"[1]. As a single, professional, thirty-year-old Australian woman, I am a youth, and I am still "playing" with the idea of a career and philosophising about the meaning of youth and feminism(s). In the meantime, many of my Asian and Pacific counterparts are grandparents supporting various generations of dependents. Their daily work is far too immediate, and precludes indulgent musings of this kind.

---

1   The UN uses the terms North and South to describe the Western, devel- oped world, and the developing world, respectively. Australia is one of few Northern countries south of the equator.

This contrast brings home the Northern and middle-class construction of youth, adolescence and childhood. In many Southern countries, these concepts are limited to the middle and upper classes. The clear exception lies in the marking of certain ages, particularly puberty, by initiation rights.

The UN defines a child as a "human being below the age of eighteen years unless, under the laws applicable to the child, majority is attained earlier" (UN: 1989). In the Western or Northern world, children are thought of as dependents, unable to earn a living. This period of their life is set aside for education and play. In the South, particularly in poor regions where literacy is low and poverty is high, a ten-year-old child may be completely emotionally and economically independent from her or his parents, with access to education and recreation limited or non-existent. While this is far from ideal for the child's psychological, intellectual and physical development, it is, however, a common way of life for millions of "children" throughout the world.

Child labour "allows" children to become youth and adults through the provision of economic resources. Contrary to popular belief, child labour is not restricted to Southern countries or the pre-industrial West. Indeed, it is on the rise in a post-industrial free-market system, with an increase in sweat shops and outworkers in all corners of the globe.

For Australia's middle and upper classes, the period of youth is lengthening, with people showing no hurry to assume adult responsibilities. This is part of a broader trend towards the ageing of youth which allows the term "young feminist" to encapsulate many hundreds of thousands of Australian women. By sheer virtue of our numbers, identification of a single, young Australian feminist voice is impossible, and the idea of an international youth-feminist-perspective is even more bizarre.

The international constructions of youth and childhood are fairly recent historical phenomena – largely a result of the global increase in mechanisation, the middle classes, and life expectancies. Although "youth" may be a fabricated, arbitrary delineation, I believe that there are issues that impact on "young women" particularly, distinguishing us from girls and older women. Certainly from the time of puberty, until society deems someone a fully responsible citizen, there are common concerns typified by issues of sexuality, access to education and employment, and the development of identity.

During the UN Youth Consultation for the Asia Pacific Region, we spent several days drafting a supplement to the regional UN document, which would be discussed at the regional governmental conference in Jakarta. At a UN meeting, language is critical, with days and sometimes weeks spent deliberating over the choice of words for regional or international documents. Regional youth lobbied for the inclusion of issues related to young women and HIV/AIDS, poverty, education and employment opportunities, sexual and reproductive health and family planning, self-esteem and consumerism, amongst others. We were taken seriously, having developed the "tools" (language) for effective lobbying. The result was a regional plan with many references to youth issues and the particular effects of more general issues on young women. This set the scene for other regional meetings, and also the Beijing Conference itself.

Prior to the Beijing Conference, the Australian Young Women's Christian Association (YWCA) received funding to identify the key concerns of young Australian women. This project, "Young Women Say", was developed and implemented by young women around the country. It involved local consultations with twenty-two groups and organisations in sixteen communities, distribution of 600 questionnaires and almost 500 street interviews. The final report states that "much social research obscures the reality of women, and in the youth sector there has been an ongoing struggle to hear the voice of young women" (YWCA: 1995, p. 1).

The "Young Women Say" project sought to document the views of young Australian women – many of which rarely receive attention in the media. When asked "what was the most important issue relating to young women?", more than half replied equal pay for equal work, followed by personal safety when out after dark, freedom of speech and respect for their views. The majority of women interviewed agreed that their lives hold more opportunities than was the case for previous generations, particularly in the paid workforce. When asked to identify the negative aspects of being a young woman, they identified their key concerns as sexism in the workplace and on the sports field, discrimination in job opportunities and sexual harassment (YWCA: 1995). The survey also suggested that women appear to be more vulnerable to media misrepresentation than older women. However, younger feminists are learning media skills and creating alternative outlets for their views, particularly through new information technologies which involve no external editing or other forms of censorship.

The results of the "Young Women Say" project highlight the differences between young Australian women and our Asian and Pacific counterparts. Unsurprisingly, they parallel many of the priorities for young women in the USA and Europe. They are very similar to the views of older Australian women, although our generation seems to have chosen different mechanisms for addressing these concerns.

The Australian preparations for the Beijing Conference brought together feminists of all ages. The mobilisation of the Australian Women's Movement at this time was astounding. I have never before seen so many national and international networks working together to agree on the international language for women's rights. In Australia, many groups actively participated in preparations, including the YWCA, the Older Women's Network (OWN), Australian Women in Sport, the Country Women's Association (CWA), the Coalition of Activist Lesbians (COAL), Amnesty International, the Girl Guides Association, and the Catholic Women's League. Young Australian women were active in most of these groups.

For me, the Beijing Women's Conference and NGO Forum were phenomenal events which assembled a rich diversity of women. Over 30 000 other women from around the world joined a conversation about women's issues and concerns. After years of preparation, Australia was represented by some 500 women.

Young women were particularly well represented at Beijing, with more youth delegates than at any UN Conference ever staged. When the proceedings began, many of the young women had already met one another and formed caucuses at regional meetings. We had developed our own Declaration and suggested language amendments to the *International Platform for Action*, the official document produced by the Conference. We worked with

women of all ages to ensure that this document represented the needs and concerns of all women, from the girl-
child to the elderly. Young women were involved in all the
activities at the conference. We led workshops, caucused
and built alliances between different groups, negotiated
with heads of state, addressed the plenary, testified as victims
of war, covered the proceedings as journalists. Young women
became a force with which to be reckoned, as we talked and
strategised on every issue, from poverty to pornography into
the early hours.

The Beijing Conference received a great deal of media
attention, much of which unfortunately, did not focus on the
issues discussed at either the Conference or the NGO Forum.
Instead, the media covered the "sensations" of Chinese
security, "clashes" between the North and South (rich and
poor) countries and the "splits" between fundamentalist and
progressive delegates on issues such as reproductive rights.

Speaking at the NGO Forum, a young Australian feminist commented on the media's portrayal of the generational divide. She argued that while young and older
women have different styles of activism, these differences
are never as stark as made out by journalists. "[T]he debate
in Australia", she continued "has been led by a school of
thought that argues that because young women aren't in
the media, therefore they aren't actively organising as
feminists in the community" (Schubert: 1995).[2] Of course,
no journalists picked up this statement!

Some older, high-profiled women aware of the media's
obsession with "big names" declined to attend the Beijing

---

2   See also Misha Schubert's Strategic Politics of Organisation pp. 217–28
    in this volume.

Conference. The American feminist icon, Gloria Steinem was one such. Instead, she wrote a letter to participants, stating that "perhaps the world media will introduce more new women to their readers and viewers at home if some of us golden oldies aren't around". Thanks Gloria, but no such luck. In fact, apart from the prominent feminists such as Betty Friedan, Bella Abzug, Jane Fonda, Hillary Clinton and Sally Field (white, middle-class, middle-aged American women), very few individual women were featured by the media.

Many Australian media commentators reflected on the differences between women's issues in the North and South. This point was made time and time again, and was typified in a cartoon showing middle-class Australian activists on one side of the Great Wall of China, and poor Chinese "peasant" women on the other. Yet, this polarisation was totally artificial and absent from both the Conference and NGO Forum. Women from different regions and cultures disagreed on some issues and agreed on many others. And wealth and class were significant axes across which positions varied, with wealthy women from Southern countries having more in common with Northern feminists, than with poor women from their own countries.

In Beijing and Huairou, feminist infighting was not the focus, in spite of what was reported in the newspapers. While I understand why the media depicted the Conference and NGO Forum in this way, I am frustrated at the misrepresentation. I guess it just doesn't sell papers to cover stories of intergenerational and international solidarity. Jackie May, an ABC correspondent, commented:

> *One of the most disheartening things for me as a journalist on location in Beijing was to be shown some of the vitriolic and misogynistic rubbish generated by male columnists in*

Australia. These so called "think" pieces refer[red] to the "middle-aged women's talk-fest" . . . I can't imagine a men's conference being similarly belittled (1996, p. 49).

This view from inside the media illustrates some of the difficulties faced by young feminist journalists. Thoughtful pieces were juxtaposed in newspapers with articles which ridiculed, scorned or trivialised the event, encouraging readers to question the legitimacy or success of the event. Calling the Conference a "middle-aged talk-fest" ignores the record-breaking presence of young women, and derides middle-aged women for their assumed domination. It also ignores the Conference's outcomes generated by workshops and plenary sessions, as well as the UN document signed by the majority of the world's nation states.

Given the overall calibre of media coverage, it is telling that the International Platform for Action should identify "increase[d] participation . . . expression and decision making in and through the media and new technologies of communication" and "promot[ion] of a balanced and non-stereotyped portrayal of women in the media" (UN: 1995, pp. 134–36).

Young feminists have a double burden in obtaining mainstream media coverage from an industry dominated by middle-aged men. Young women's feminist issues will not be accurately portrayed in our newspapers, magazines and television shows until more feminists, who are supportive of other women, gain access to decision-making in the Australian media industry.

In Beijing, I came to understand the importance of working towards feminist goals at an international level. Young Australian women lobbied effectively to establish an international legal framework for women's human rights. We focused our attention on the rights that Australian women have fought for during three generations: the right to vote, the right to equal pay, the right to education, and the right to be free from violence and harassment. The "Beijing experience" internationalised and strengthened Australia's feminist movements. We learned from the experience of other women, and they learned from ours. This was especially so for young women. Importantly, we developed relationships and connections with women from around the world. And, in this age of increasing technology, these links are being maintained as we continue our lobbying and campaigning.

If only because of our sheer numbers, young women are becoming a powerful force. Today, half the world's population is under twenty-five – youth represent a majority. Increasingly, the social and political agenda will be influenced by young minds. In Beijing, you couldn't help but stand back and be inspired, watching them take the floor – articulating the issues of the future and moulding the agenda – across boundaries of nations and ages.

What You See is *Not* What You Get

Vivienne Wynter

> On this island where we live, keeping what we do not tell, we
> have found the infinite variety of Woman. On the Mainland,
> Woman is largely extinct in all but a couple of obvious forms.
> She is still cultivated as a cash crop but is nowhere to be
> found growing wild
> JEANNETTE WINTERSON: 1993, P. 419.

When I was fourteen and living on the Gold Coast in the early 1980s my younger sister and I starved ourselves by placing bets with each other so that the first who ate on a particular day had to pay the other five bucks. Our lives were dominated by the drive to be thin. Feeling hungry was synonymous with virtue. It was by being thin, blonde (bleached in my case) and tanned, that we avoided the worst tag of all in Gold Coast vernacular – a "bush-pig". In our campaign to be thin, blonde and tanned, we were determined to be like the chicks in the surf magazines and Brian Rochford bikini ads.

Achieving "the look" was no mean feat for me. Coming from a Scottish-English background with naturally red hair, freckled skin and child-bearing hips, I was a natural candidate for bush-pig status. But by starving, exercising, bleaching and depilating myself to within an inch of my life, I managed to be something different from my natural self and escaped derision from the surfie groups that ruled the Gold Coast. I even managed to snare one of the cutest members of the local surfie gang as a boyfriend.

But there was a price for reaching the elusive status of beach-babe. Beach-babes had smooth, tanned, baby-oiled skin, fluffy blonde hair, glossy lips, firm, round bottoms and breasts, and sassy, cute personalities. Beach-babes were mainly decorative. Industries were built around us. Together, pharmaceutical companies producing diet pills and fake tans, solariums, beauty clinics, hairdressers, producers of film clips for bands like Australian Crawl and Duran Duran and of ads for Kentucky Fried Chicken all cheered for the beach-babe because they all stood to gain.

For someone like me living on the Gold Coast, things weren't so glossy. If you happened to fit the popular mould "naturally" you entered happily into the garden of acceptance and status. By transforming myself into a beach-babe, I managed to pass as a desirable female. But inside, I knew I wasn't really what they saw, and I lived in fear of being found out. The intense pressure on young women to conform to the popular ideal often meant that we had to disown, reject, or discard major parts of ourselves – a process which can have damaging and enduring psychological consequences. I only managed to pull it off by consciously disowning my natural self and putting on another costume. This metamorphosis was almost like pulling on a new skin and it was infused with anxiety and self-doubt. And this process continues today. In the 1990s, while the music, the styles and the players may have changed, teenage girls are still under both subtle and obvious pressure from the popular media and their peers to fit an ideal image of woman. Magazines for young women freely admit to conducting surveys about their readers' fears and anxieties about their appearance so they can pass them on to their advertisers. The media still promotes painfully thin women with abnormally large eyes and lips, and midriffs so tight you could play them like bongo drums.

It wasn't until I began university that I felt liberated enough to be myself. There I found women and men who encouraged and even celebrated ways of being a woman that went beyond the stereotypes. What a relief!

It was that exhilarating experience of liberation that led me to "look back in anger" at my school days and to decide that I wanted things to be different for the next generation. I chose the media as the focal point for my efforts. My activism began with a letter to my university newspaper, criticising a boys' college magazine which was holding a spot-the-college-girl-being-dragged-off-at-a-ball competition.

As a journalism student, I remember being perplexed at the news values of the media which were often different from the values we were being taught. I remember writing a story showing, for the first time, that more Aboriginal women were killed by their partners on Far North Queensland than there were black deaths in custody throughout Australia. With a Royal Commission into black deaths in custody at that time, I thought this was a major story and expected the mainstream media to pick it up. But the papers

I sent it to weren't interested. Later in my career, editors told me quietly, "people just don't want to know about that stuff".

It was while I was studying that I decided I didn't accept the explicit values of the media where youth, beauty and money were shrines while a range of other stories were not told or chased. For several years now, I have been a member of MediaSwitch, an organisation which monitors the portrayal of women in the media. As the group's media spokeswoman, I often give the example of my coming of age on the Gold Coast to explain why I am a feminist. Looking back on my time on the Gold Coast, I realise that anger at my limited choices then, has fuelled many of my attitudes now. The personal is political.

My feminist activity has predominantly focused on media issues. One thing I have in common with the advertising industry and the mainstream media is a strong belief in the potent power of images and language to structure our desires and values. I profoundly believe that the dominant public cultural perceptions of women have a direct effect on relationships between women and men, between women and women and between women and children. Compare the media's treatment of violence against Aboriginal women from their own partners to its coverage of attacks on white women by strangers. The media is much less outraged by the former and so we see continuing campaigns for more police on the street in urban areas while government responses to the problems of violence on black communities remain woefully inadequate.

We cannot avoid being affected by a culture which continues to define issues such as childcare, the environment, education, discrimination, aged-care, domestic violence and welfare as "soft" news of low priority; while issues such as economics, sport, politics, defence and development are defined as "hard" news with the right of way over competing stories. I defy anyone to live in but not be affected by a media culture which subtly says to women, "if you want front page attention you must either look like Elle McPherson or be as shocking as Pauline Hanson".

The women in MediaSwitch operate from the premise that the images, language, portrayals and implicit messages used in the news media, in advertising, in movies, magazines and on the Internet often fail to represent fairly the reality and diversity of women's lives and roles. While it has become popular to argue that misrepresentation is no longer an issue, research shows that the majority of women are unhappy with the way they are portrayed in the media. In 1993, Southdown Research Services found that sixty-two per cent of women think the media does not accurately reflect the lives of women in the 1990s. Despite this amazing statistic, advertisers and the news media continue to resist change, arguing that only a small minority of women find their products objectionable. So, we continue to see products advertised with women draped on them, page-three girls and the editing out of women who do not fit into a size ten. Women and women's issues are edited out of the majority of news and current affairs in the print and broadcast media. In 1993 the Office of the Status of Women[1] found that women were featured in news stories only eighteen per cent of the time and that only twenty-seven per cent of newspaper

---

1   *Women in the Media: The National Working Party on the Portrayal of Women in the Media.* Office of the Status of Women. (1993).

by-lines and picture captions mentioned women. Yet, there are slightly more women than men in Australia. So why then do women only "take up" a quarter of the media space?

As media workers, women are even more under-represented than they are as media subjects. Women fill less than a quarter of senior, editorial or presenting positions in the media. Of 270 feature films made in Australia during the previous decade, only twenty-one were made by women. In commercial radio, women are rarely, if ever, permitted to host morning current affairs talk-show programs. To my knowledge there is no capital city commercial radio station with a solo female presenting the prime-time breakfast radio program. Men are the voice of authority in news and pro-grams and advertising sections of most radio stations. Several studies of radio advertising have found that fewer than twenty per cent of ads use a female voice-over.

Just as research shows that boys dominate space and time in the playground and the classroom, men dominate space in the media. Making matters worse, they are not content with monopolising media time. They also use that space to define how women should look and behave. They impose value judgements about what is important and what is trivial.

MediaSwitch aims to educate media consumers on being active participants in the production of media and cultural messages, rather than passive, (if sometimes angry) con-sumers. We conduct community and school training to inform people how they can engage with the media through journalists, editors and advertisers. We refuse to accept a one-way relationship where the media holds up a badly distorted mirror to society. We want to demystify that powerful and often infuriating monster called the mass media. We aim to give women confidence to "report back" to the media supported by their consumer power. We demand honest, varied representations of women. We ask for media workplaces to be fair and friendly to women, so that we also have direct opportunities to affect what goes *in to* the media.

Interest in the issues around women in the media peaked in the mid-1980s and although government funding for research has declined under the rise of conservative state and federal governments, there continues to be wide interest in media representation today. But the down-side of the mainstreaming of the issue is the growing argument that it is oppressive and patronising toward women to "study" them as subjects in the media. No sooner had the issue of women and the media begun to receive serious recognition and funding than the "new" feminists began undermining and denigrating this work.

Catherine Lumby, a high-profile critic of feminist activity, devotes her 1997 book, *bad girls, the media, sex and feminism in the 90s* to criticising feminist analysis of the media, declaring it passé. She depicts such critiques as "puritanical and outmoded, not recognising the ease with which today's young women engage with the media or indeed the aplomb with which these women practise feminism and manage their sexuality" (1997, back cover).

She shoots down the work of feminist activists in the media for allegedly treating other women patronisingly because "feminists are ultimately forced to argue they simply know better than the average woman – that they've discovered the 'truth'" (1997, p. 13). Lumby describes feminist campaigns against "sexist" advertisements as simplistic:

> *Knee-jerk claims that an image is "sexist" are rarely backed up with coherent arguments. Prominent feminist politicians and public figures seeking broadcast airtime routinely get away with assertions that an ad or program purveys "negative" or "degrading" images of women party because the media has been so quick to give feminists the moral high ground* (1997, p. xiv).

This criticism reveals a common misconception about the work of feminists in the media. For example, MediaSwitch rarely describes an image or program as "sexist" – the debate has gone beyond recourse to that simple tag. MediaSwitch does not routinely call for certain images to be banned, nor do we claim to decipher or translate "the truth" of images or language. The bulk of feminist work in the media is concerned with educating interested people and groups on how to engage with the media to ensure that there is more fairness and accuracy in its coverage. For example, MediaSwitch entered into public debate when *Dolly* magazine selected an extremely thin thirteen-year-old girl as the winner of its 1997 cover-girl contest. We commented that it was a shame that the most popular magazine on the market for young girls continues to laud only painfully thin, very young women. Doesn't *Dolly* owe its readers a duty of care to promote a diversity of ideal images, especially with the chronic problems of anorexia, bulimia and other eating disorders among young women?

MediaSwitch campaigns also lobby for positive change. Just as constant negative portrayals of Aboriginal people in the media feed racist agendas, so too, demeaning and trivialising treatment of women in the media reduces our value and reinforces stereotypical attitudes to women in society at large. These values have begun a slow shift away from obsessive preoccupation with physical attractiveness. The balance between women's achievements and concerns and men's are improving. We are now living in an era where men and women are learning more about the opposite gender. However, I do argue for a bit of positive discrimination for women during the period of transition. We have heard, seen and watched men for a long time now. We know what men think is a desirable woman. The time is right to ask, more often, what women think is good in the media. Good at work? Good at home? Good on TV? Good in bed?

Options will continue to be fairly limited for some women as long as the process of editing out dissenting voices from the media continues as part of a conscious power play between different social groups. While I wrote this article, newspapers around Australia continued to give women significant coverage, predominantly in roles as mothers or sex symbols. In my local paper, I learned about the first woman to pilot a chopper around the world in a story headlined "Granny Takes Round Trip". A Senior journalist in a Sunday tabloid guffawed into the pages about keeping "abreast" of the new styles in women's underwear. A size-fourteen model was banned from 1997 Fashion Week parades. The Australian Sports Commission said that the only way women athletes seem able to get attention from an uninterested media is to sell sex by posing in soft-porn photos. Individually these scenarios may seem harmless, however, the effect of collectively editing out women in all their roles, shapes and attitudes is somewhat more foreboding. This reinforces dominant public perceptions of women as fishwives (Pauline Hanson), goddesses (Elle Macpherson) or nymphs (Dannii Minogue). There are exceptions – Democrats Deputy Leader, Natasha Stott Despoja is one – but my goal is for a media culture where high profile, intelligent, respected women are not interesting exceptions.

It is up to media consumers to let practitioners know they are tired of journalists, advertisers and film-makers who legitimise the attitudes and beliefs of the dominant groups, often by silencing others. Only if consumers demand better standards will we see a more responsible and accountable media, one which moves away from cliched images and language to embrace a more inclusive, diverse and fair approach to portraying both men and women. This is the type of feminism I'm interested in – one that throws out the old measurements of women by their attractiveness and men by their prowess, and recognises the fluid attributes of each gender and values them equally.

It is not beyond conception. Formula journalism could be refreshed with new approaches to asking questions and telling stories. Media consumers could be surprised by unconventional images illustrating stories and advertisements. This approach could invigorate the mass media and not before time, because white, male dominance of the media creates a mono-culture of sameness that is boring as well as inaccurate. It is not impossible for media practitioners to find ways to value the contributions made by women who are not decorative in a conventional sense. For example, the wisdom and strength of an Aboriginal elder who holds her community together through grievous alcohol abuse could earn similar recognition as the Aboriginal student who gets her picture on the front page of the paper because she got a gig with French *Vogue*.

I believe any analysis of feminism, society and the media which argues that the entire social structure has completely reversed in a few decades is narrow-sighted. While it is valid, and indeed necessary, to critique feminist practice, throwing out the feminist baby with the bathwater would be a catastrophic loss at this time in history.

In 1996 *DIY Feminism* set out to define the mood and aspirations of women in the 1990s. It looks disparagingly at the philosophy and techniques of the Feminist Movement. "The generational shift in feminism is allied to a do-it-yourself style and philosophy characteristic of youth culture", Bail says in the introduction to *DIY*. She describes modern women as:

> Riot grrrls, guerrilla girls, net chicks, cyber chix, geekgirls, tank girls, super girls, action girls, deep girls (1996, p. 3).

Very peppy stuff, *DIY* seems to present feminism almost as an optional life-style for young women to put on and discard at their whim. While a couple of the chapters in *DIY* advocate feminist agitation and strategy, the overall tone of the book suggests we should "groove up". I get the impression from *DIY* that anyone suffering sexual harassment should whip out an AK47 and nuke the guy and walk away laughing and if you're feeling a bit intimidated about penetrating a male-dominated field such as journalism, sport, politics or business, you should just "get over it". If it were as simple as that we probably would have done so by now!

My experience tells me that this is not the case. My career as a journalist has been almost totally dependent on the kindness and patronage of men. Male lecturers and tutors at university were my inspiration, taking the time to mentor me, giving me confidence and skills. Male employers "gave" me all my jobs and male mentors taught me how to use computers and write and broadcast news and how to have "tough bark on me" for this male environment.

With honourable exceptions, I rarely meet women senior and secure enough in their positions to reach out the friendly hand of mentorship. Mentoring programs for women are only beginning to emerge and there is a long way to go yet before women enjoy the same level of patronage and encouragement at work, particularly in media workplaces, as men. In light of my experience and observation of the inroads made by women thus far, I see as gravely premature any canvassing of the DIY approach as the alternative style for feminism to the collective, principled movements of the 1960s and 1970s.

Books like *DIY Feminism* and *bad girls* concern me because they generalise the gains won mainly by young, white, middle-class women. They assume that the whole gender stands on an equal footing. The fact that Aboriginal women have only begun to make (albeit rare) appearances in capital city newspapers, TV and radio bulletins is stark evidence that certain voices are deliberately edited out of popular culture even if young white girls are getting a decent guernsey.

Bail and Lumby's commentaries appear to have applied the fashionable concept of economic rationalism to feminism, hypothesising that all women are free to "help themselves" to a serving of liberation if they could just get motivated. I see women's equality coming from massive cultural and institutional change that would empower all women to "get themselves some liberation".

When I look back at the fourteen-year-old, Gold Coast girl starving herself, busy conforming to an impossible ideal, I think of the Jeanette Winterson quote that opens this chapter. Woman is grown as a cash crop on the mainland, she writes, but "is nowhere to be found growing wild".

I want to urge that fourteen-year-old Gold Coast me and fourteen-year-old girls today to give up the exhausting and self-defeating work of meeting impossible ideals and "grow wild". And when all kinds of women and girls take their places as valued, visible and influential members of the public culture, maybe then I will agree with the DIY feminists. Meantime there's still work to do.

For more information about MediaSwitch, write to:
MediaSwith (QLD) Inc., PO Box 49, THE GRANGE, QLD 4051.

Reading Magazines

Samantha Brazel

The setting for my chapter is the office of *Who Weekly*, a popular weekly magazine published in Australia, where I am employed as a copy editor. The weekly deadline makes it a fast-paced, dynamic place of work, and my work includes cutting stories to fit page layouts and editing them for correct grammar and expression. In many ways I take on the role of the ultimate reader, to ensure the story makes sense.

Traditionally, feminist analysis of the mass-magazine industry concentrates on stereotypical representation of women. Feminists argue that these magazines and their advertisers present women in a simplistic and idealistic manner. They criticise content that focuses on women's appearance and their relationships or articles offering tips – sometimes explicitly – on fulfilling traditional expectations of women as perfect wife and mother, and as paid workers in a limited range of occupations.

That said, it may surprise some people to learn that magazine publishing is a female-dominated industry. This is reflected at *Who Weekly* in a 3:1 female to male ratio on the Sydney-based editorial team of editors, writers, designers, photo editors and researchers. Some people would then point out that most magazine publishers are men, and suggest it is they who wield ultimate power. But while publishers do have power over budgets, and even over the editorial direction of magazines, it would be rare to find a publisher in touch with the day-to-day decision making that takes place on a weekly publication. And it is absurd to think that they might affect each and every story in a publication. It is also important to recognise that many magazines aim to attract a female audience; an audience that presumably will not accept (read: buy) content that does not reflect their attitudes, interests and views.

An insight into the type of magazine *Who Weekly* is can be garnered from its editorial objectives:

> *Our premise is that people are vitally interested in other people, whether they be extraordinary individuals or ordinary people caught up in extraordinary situations. Each week we focus on popular culture's active personalities – stars, newcomers and bit-players – drawing our subjects from the worlds of entertainment and the arts, as well as from real-life crime, disasters and other breaking news. We try to get behind public facades to the real person; to fill in personal backgrounds, flesh out characters and opinions, and reveal what makes people tick. We try to capture in words and pictures as much intimate*

detail as we can, but with compassion and sensitivity. We hope
to be fair, informative and entertaining; never cruel or awe-
struck. We aim to offer fresh appraisal, to ask, "Who is this
person?" and to give an honest, up-to-date answer (Statement
to the Australian Society for Magazine Editors).

The other objective, of course, is to sell magazines and
make a profit. In order to meet *Who Weekly*'s editorial and
business goals many decisions are made about what our
readers will find interesting. What will ensure that they
buy this issue? There is no tried and true formula for
success but ultimately each issue is made up of stories that
reflect the objectives above. Our aim is to present stories in
such a way as to attract readers/buyers. So the *Who Weekly*
editorial team constantly aspires to interest its potential
audience – from the all important choice of cover, to the
magazine's content and story subjects, and down to the
headlines for individual stories. Many opinions are heard
in the process of making these decisions and this is central
to my excavation of feminist strategy in my workplace. The
answers to what will work each week depend on who's asking. The result for each individual story can differ according
to who is choosing the story, writing it and who has the final
say about the words that go to print.

As more young, thoughtful women gain positions at the
magazine, they affect the way *Who Weekly* presents itself.
We suggest stories that interest us and suggest changes to
stories, and our opinions are heard and discussed. Because
our opinions can and are often seen to reflect those held by
readers (sixty per cent of whom are women), our voices
have more power than young voices in other occupations.
Of course, a story will not be published simply because it

"interests" us. There must be a perceived wider interest. For example, stories are rejected because they are not perceived to be relevant Australia-wide. In such cases the business consideration of national circulation directs the choice. Another consideration stems from the magazine's editorial objectives: stories are almost always based on a person; issue-based stories must have a human angle. However, it is the judgment calls made during daily meetings of the editorial team and presided over by the editor, which ultimately determine content. In real terms, the more people within the editorial team lobbying for a story, or a change to a story, the more likely it is to make it into the magazine.

At *Who Weekly*, there are no "feminist" content policies – and let's face it the magazine is not set up to serve women or explicitly champion women's causes or debate women's issues. It is because of this that I have chosen to discuss how feminist ideas affect the magazine. While feminist organisations offer valuable services and opportunities, feminism should not be considered as merely "other"; or as something that only exists outside the mainstream, or separate from informal, everyday work practices. In fact, for feminism to have truly succeeded as a political force for change it must become part of mainstream life: feminist ideas must be accepted as natural, everywhere.

Because of my interest and studies in feminism, when I work on stories at *Who Weekly*, I read from a feminist perspective. I particularly notice content that I think is sexist. Many things I notice, go unnoticed by others, however, when they are pointed out and discussed it seems obvious to everyone to make changes to the articles. Sometimes I rely on arguments of repetition when suggesting changes rather than sexism; space and word count rather than a desire to eliminate sexist detail. These are the tools of my job. Whatever the tactic the result is the same: the sexist content is omitted. I'm sure some of my colleagues would respond badly if I constantly accused them of sexism. I prefer to think, and my experiences bear this out, that they are looking at the text differently. It is the writer's job to create strong descriptions that evoke mental pictures and feelings; through my job as a copy editor I act as a conduit between writer and reader, by discussing my responses to the way a story is told.

At base, most feminist practice is about revealing the ways in which men and women are treated differently and then attempting to correct this imbalance. It may be " just a magazine article", however, the more often *Who Weekly* treats men and women similarly in stories, the more feminist it becomes. I have seen the influence of feminist ideas in some subtle and some startling ways while working at the magazine and my experiences are an example of the ways in which feminists in not-so-feminist occupations can make a difference for women. Let me relate a couple of examples.

Who Weekly often runs book extracts accompanied by an interview with the author. *It Could Have Been You* by English fashion buyer Merlyn Nuttall was reviewed in this way in early 1997 (Nuttall and Morrison: 1997). Nuttall was the victim of an horrific rape, after which her attacker attempted to murder her. She wrote "the book I needed to read after my own attack" with a view to helping other rape victims. At the time, Nuttall and her book were receiving a great deal of publicity in the UK, not only because her story of survival was extraordinary, but also because in 1996 she had won a record compensation claim (AU$162 000). This claim was awarded just prior to the changes to British law which capped the amount rape victims could claim. A male employee at *Who Weekly* in the UK thought this eloquent and obviously very strong woman would make a good story subject, so he organised an interview, obtained rights to the book and compiled an extract. The edited extract he sent to Sydney comprised Nuttall's compelling and horrific description of her rape, which included her abduction in broad daylight, rape, garrotting and beating and her eventual escape after being set on fire by her attacker who believed her dead.

When I first read the extract my reaction was almost physical; it upset – even frightened – me. Juxtaposed with the book's title, *It Could Happen to You*, Nuttall's account was distressing; it positioned me as the potential "you". This had been pitched as a story of a woman who wanted to help other rape victims, but this was not my idea of a road to recovery. I was bewildered by the extract. Was it a collection of "my rape was better/worse than yours" stories? Perhaps, more importantly, I could not understand *Who Weekly*'s interest in running such a disturbing piece. I immediately expressed my concern to the deputy editor, but she felt unable to take any action as neither of us had read the book. She suggested that I contact the male employee in London who had compiled the extract. I was so concerned that I didn't want to wait until the time differences coincided for a discussion before I tried to find out more about the book. If it was left too late, the magazine's deadline could well prevent anyone from changing the story.

It turned out that the description of the rape was one chapter of a diary-style book, which also discussed the aftermath of the attack: the hospital experience (including Nuttall's reprimand to a nurse not to clean her hands until they had been swabbed for physical evidence), the police investigation, Nuttall's testimony which assisted in imprisoning her attacker and her recovery both physically and psychologically from the assault.

A copy of the book was obtained and another discussion took place. The solution offered was the inclusion within the article of a box with a point-form list of things to do after an attack using information provided in the book's appendix. I remained concerned that the extract represented a limited expression of the book's content – and one which emphasised the rape rather than the recovery. At the same time my colleagues were concerned that resolving my misgivings would entail too much extra work. I was asked to compile the box. Instead, I compiled an alternative extract. The extract still included the rape, but it was cut by half in order to make way for parts of Nuttall's story describing her recovery. *Who Weekly* chose to run this version.

The original extract had ended with Nuttall, bleeding profusely as she escaped the burning building where she had been raped and collapsed on the road. Now the extract ended with Nuttall looking toward the future:

> *I have tried so many times to analyse why I feel strong, and I have come to the conclusion that I, unlike many other victims of violent crime, have never felt (or been made to feel) the slightest bit of guilt. The fact that I thought I was going to die on that day has changed my whole outlook on life. Far from feeling embittered and angry about what happened to me, I treat each day as a bonus* (Nuttall and Morrison: 1987, p. 52).

For me this was an important victory. It became a story of survival, rather than a voyeuristic account of a woman's worst nightmare.

Looking back, the male editor of the original extract had prioritised dramatic impact over context. When he read *It Could Have Been You*, he was most compelled by the vividly recounted rape chapter. His extract concentrated on Nuttall's "action-packed escape" from death. He didn't read it and put himself in the picture, as I, a young woman automatically did. How could he? The book was not aimed at him. It could not have been him and so the description of the rape did not provoke fear in him. He could not see that relating the rape alone would leave a female reader deeply affected. From a female perspective, Nuttall's victory was not physical survival (which was, indeed, a remarkable feat) but emotional survival and recovery.

The decision to change the extract was an acknowledgment of a feminist perspective at the magazine. When offered the second extract, the managers quickly accepted it, and most importantly, I think the story was better for it. On a simpler level, the extract now represented the book more accurately. Unable to see the wood for the trees, the male editor had not seen the story for the drama of its beginning. And perhaps more importantly, the original extract did not reflect the author's intention to advise, guide and to support victims of rape.

There are many other subtle ways in which stories are altered in a feminist manner. For example, *People Weekly*, *Who Weekly*'s sister magazine in the US, carried a story on Hollywood Mothers. The article included a picture caption that read: "Post-partum depression isn't an option for such sexy moms as Whitney Houston, Madonna and super-model Nikki Taylor" (1997, May 26, p. 3). *Who Weekly* picked the story to run in Australia but the caption was changed after a number of staff – including men – pointed out that post-partum depression is a medical condition that affects some women after they have given birth, not a life-style choice, and secondly, that fame is certainly no antidote. Later, the Australian decision to change the caption was vindicated when the US publication received many letters from readers offended by the caption:

> *Your statement about post-partum depression was not only ignorant but insensitive to those of us who have suffered through the ordeal. It wasn't an "option" for me but a reality* (People Weekly: June 16, 1997, p. 1).

> *I wish I had known earlier that my wife had a choice as she suffered through nearly three years of post-partum depression following two pregnancies. I will surely have to chastise her for making such an irrational choice! Your casual portrayal of this condition it irresponsible and reprehensible* (People Weekly: June 16, 1997, p. 1).

The writer's casual choice of words and, conceivably, lack of research, painted a picture that offended. The frivolous tone did not alter the offence, which was avoided in Australia when *Who Weekly* staff read the caption and understood it to be glib, incorrect and especially offensive to women who have suffered from post-partum depression. This incident only reaffirmed my experience that writers are often unaware of some of the connotations that their choice of words can convey. In a smaller way this example echoes the first.

Perhaps inadvertently, writers often treat men and women differently in their stories. In a piece about a crime in America, a female district attorney's comments about the case were prefaced with her title and a description of her as the mother of two young sons. *Who Weekly* staff pointed out that if we had quoted, for example, the NSW Police Commissioner, Peter Ryan, we would not think to add that he was a father. We would be interested solely in his professional opinion. When the story was printed in Australia, the article simply described her as a DA. In this case, the writer probably thought the personal description added depth to the DA's comments. In fact, it was irrelevant to her professional assessment.

Often when writing a story about a woman, a writer will focus unduly on a physical description. They will not just describe her appearance in detail, but continue to refer to her appearance throughout the article. On a number of occasions when I have pointed out what I interpret as excessive detail about a subject's appearance, repetitive references have been cut. My argument for reducing the attention on the physical is not just that it is sexist, but also that it can detract from the woman's actions or opinions and that it is perhaps a waste of space that could be used to reveal further or more interesting information.

These examples represent a couple of my experiences of being strategically feminist at *Who Weekly*. However, I do not wish to appear as the lone feminist voice at the magazine. At *Who Weekly* there are many other women who, in doing their jobs, also act as feminists, because of the feminist values they bring to the interpretation of the material they are working with. I'm sure there are also other young women in magazines and elsewhere who have similar responses, but are not yet sufficiently confident to speak out, and put the arguments before their colleagues. I hope that seeing others debate these issues gives them confidence, so that next time, they too can take on problematic aspects of a story or situation.

In many ways, my anecdotes describe only very small successes, but these successes add up, and their positive effect expands from sentences, to stories, to entire magazines. As more stories benefit from being produced with women readers in mind, more care is now taken to approach women's experiences seriously, and represent them as fully as possible. In magazines, male and female subjects must be treated similarly and language must be used carefully because words will mean different things to different readers. As more young women gain positions in organisations such as *Who Weekly*, more and more women are affecting the telling of the stories. It must follow that the more young women, who have grown up in a society which takes certain feminist principles about equality, the law and sex for granted, and who are involved in telling stories, the more these stories will reflect these values, ideas and perspectives.

The Strategic Politics of Organisation

Misha Schubert

From the Girlpower Diary.

April 1997

86 Nicholson Street, Fitzroy

> *A gang of twentysomethings, mostly women, sit sprawled around a lounge room littered with pizza boxes and Diet Coke cans. This time the occasion isn't Melrose Night. They've been invited to discuss the government's Constitutional Convention on the Republic.*
>
> *In this room are the political upstarts who will soon form their own youth ticket for the event and take on the well-resourced forces of the babyboomers.*
>
> *The discussion switches from small talk into strategy.*
>
> *"Do you have any idea how many votes we'll need to get elected?" somone asks rhetorically. "At the bare minimum, 100 000."*
>
> *There's a long pause as the scope of the dream sets in.*
>
> *"Shit." someone mutters.*
>
> *But within weeks a campaign has taken shape – focus groups will research views and test opinions, we'll build a web site, start fundraising through events and grant applications, complete email and snail mail contact lists, generate media coverage, enlist some prominent supporters, recruit like crazy, train volunteers, run a public forum and make a television advertisement.*
>
> *All in a day's work for the daughters of modern feminism.*

It was no accident that a network of young women had the political vision and the skills to run an independent youth ticket for the nation's Constitutional Convention in the late 1990s. Our capacity to do so is attests to the progress of feminism.

As we gathered a group of campaigners and started planning a political presence, we drew from precocious experience. Some came with a history of running student election campaigns at university, others with management skills gleaned as volunteers in women's organisations like the YWCA and the Women's Electoral Lobby. Some were communications kids – students of the media and public relations, while others came to their first political experience armed only with almost boundless energy. Across this diversity, we were unified by a vision of political participation. We knew the significance of the opportunity presented by the Convention, both as an historical event and as a forum in which to train young women in electoral politics.

Our political instinct for the task was no coincidence. More than any generation of women before us, the "FemXers" were groomed to dream audaciously and to realise our ambitions. We were schooled to think, plan and manage our way into political power, thanks largely to our mothers' groundbreaking activism. We are the daughters of modern feminism the students and recipients of its evolution. And now we have a role as feminism's strategists.

We grew up watching our mothers lobby for public policy reform and battle inequality in the paid work force. My mother was a teacher and resigned voluntarily during her pregnancy with me, before her marriage eleven months following my birth. Had she not done so, she would have been forced to resign, only to be offered reinstatement as a casual employee after her wedding. Around the same time, her friend Charmaine McEachern, wanted to keep her maiden name post-marriage, but was informed by the education department that she would only be paid if she used her married name.

Teachers like my mother and Charmaine educated my generation of girls, and their feminist values and working-class roots imbued us with a strong social justice ethic. Their intellects won them teaching bursaries and, later, middle-class salaries, making them supremely conscious of the capacity of formal education to enhance fortunes and bring about social change.

My mother's story is fairly typical. Born at Ceduna on the far-west coast of South Australia, she was the second of four girls in an impoverished post-war family. Her father had returned from the Second World War with advanced alcoholism, leaving the family for periods of time until his final departure before my mother turned five. My grandmother lost the family farm as a result of their alcohol-related debt, subsequently moving to a rental house and then her mother's ramshackle, three-room house on the outskirts of town. At the time, "deserted wives" had to wait seven years to qualify for a pension. Until then, they were reliant on the goodwill of extended family for support. An enormously resourceful woman, my grandmother fed her four daughters by growing vegetables, keeping a milking cow, obtaining ration coupons and by washing clothes and baking cakes.

At the age of fifteen my mother boarded with her aunt and uncle in Adelaide, while completing her school Leaving Honours and then attending Adelaide Teachers' College. While at school, she was made a counter-offer of a Commonwealth Scholarship, which might have allowed her to study medicine or law, but it paid less than the (still modest) teaching bursary, so she declined it. Looking back, she says there was pressure to "settle" with teaching; a "don't get too big for your boots" attitude toward her advancement.

Many aspects of my mother's story are representative of

her feminist generation. Women of her generation were advocates, counsellors and community-builders. They ran committees, lobbied for political reform and fostered the confidence and ambition of the young women they taught. If they felt that their own ambition had been stifled, they were determined that their daughters would not be discouraged. These women built a broadly accepted platform and created a culture in which feminism could come of age.

I look particularly at the remarkable commitment of my friend and mentor Val Byth and wonder whether we will have feminists like her in the future. Val spent nearly sixteen years as the full-time, unpaid coordinator of WEL in Victoria. She managed a team of volunteer women who had specific portfolio expertise, coordinating their responses to policy or legislation as the need arose. To do this, she searched for, and recruited feminists who worked in areas from health funding to aged-care, violence to education. She facilitated their commentary by publishing articles and arranging ministerial lobbying visits. She wrote an extensive monthly newsletter which was the definitive guide to feminist issues and events, a "must read" which allowed busy women to keep up to date. She is possibly the best net-worker I have ever seen, attending innumerable functions and managing to collect allies among politicians and bureaucrats, activists and philanthropists. With a particular interest in the involvement of young women and rural women, Val has personally encouraged many of us to assist in sustaining a feminist involvement alongside other de-manding life pressures.

Perhaps Val's greatest talent lies in "keeping track" of women who are needed for the cause. The first time I met her was during my time as the Women's Officer at the National Union of Students in August, 1993. We said we'd stay in touch. After I completed my frantic term in this position, I took some time to study and vowed not to get involved in activism again until I'd had a proper rest.

About a year later, Val called. "You've had a rest, " she said, "and it's time to come back". She had tracked down my new telephone number through my student feminist networks in Adelaide, where I had lived years before. Val invited me to speak at a conference WEL were organising about young women and feminism; and so began my immersion in the broader Women's Movement.

During the following six years, I juggled paid work as a marketing consultant, my media studies at RMIT, commitments to the NUS, WEL, the YWCA, the UN Conference on Women in Beijing, and a social life. Having an understanding employer was the only way that this was possible. My boss viewed my extracurricular activities as a sign of my value, and agreed to flexible arrangements which allowed me to disappear for three hours in the middle of the day and make up the work time after hours; conditions which were unlikely to be replicated elsewhere. But like all involvements I suspect that feminism is ultimately cyclical. Since starting a demanding new job in print journalism, I have struggled to keep the balance of commitments, knowing that my employer has the greater call on my time and energy. I expect to make my contribution by writing feminist opinion pieces for a while, with organisational commitments becoming an after hours concern.

Few of us have employers who allow activism to be an intergrated part of our work day. So the day-to-day activities of organised feminism tend to be run by paid part-time staff in women's organisations with a small, committed volunteer base. Some might argue that a lack of time or resources is nothing new for the Women's Movement. But feminism's achievements have been disproportionate to its resources. It still amazes me to hear the stories behind impressive public policy wins, especially where a campaign was conducted by just a handful of well-organised women. Feminists have achieved a great deal for many women in a relatively short period of time.

It is because of its phenomenal success that feminism has begun to be viewed as an institutional power. Having permeated the bureaucracy and academies, feminist thought has in many instances become common sense, rather than radical doctrine. It is now accepted that women should not be forced to resign from their jobs when they marry, should not have to endure domestic violence, nor should they be subjected to sexual harassment at work. High profile Australian feminists like Patricia Turner at ATSIC,[1] Sandra Yates at Saatchi and Saatchi and Ann Sherry at Westpac hold positions of significant influence in the public and private sectors. Feminist authors like Anne Summers and Helen Garner are among the babyboomers who exercise clout in the world of publishing and ideas.

With this level of influence, it is unsurprising that critics from inside and outside the Movement have begun to generalise about the capacities, potential and failings of organised feminism. Recently, I was in the news room after

---

1   ATSIC is the acronym for the Aboriginal and Torres Strait Islander Com-
    mission, a national statutory body set up in Australia in 1989 by the
    Hawke Labor Government to administer funding and oversee programs
    to improve the quality of life for Aboriginal and Torres Strait Islanders.

the committal hearing of a man charged with murdering his girlfriend's child. Media reports portrayed the accused's girlfriend as a deeply insecure young woman who lacked opportunities, ambition and independence. A senior writer in the bureau looked at the article and said to me (as a public feminist, you are invariably responsible for the entire history of feminism) "Feminism has done nothing for women like her". I thought about the comment for a while before I responded, saying it was a tough call to blame feminism for what it hasn't done, as though it were some kind of omnipresent institutional force. This construction of feminism assumes levels of resources and coordination which simply do not exist. A grassroots movement is seldom centrally coordinated or planned. Individual women tend to work on the issues they know locally or personally, not as a matter of self-interest, but rather because of expertise. Many women feel (rightly) uncomfortable about advocating for others where it may be seen as paternalistic. Thus, the more recent approach has been to provide personal or organisational support to women of diverse backgrounds as they advocate their own issues.

So, to the critics I return the challenge. If you want feminism to be or do something it is not, then the best way to make it happen is to take up the issue yourself. Feminism, is not, despite its impact, an institution. It is a loose-knit collection of non-government organisations and individual women, most of whom could do with an injection of time, money and energy. The most effective way to influence the priorities of the Movement is to throw yourself into the fray or assist others who do so with time and/or resources.

Meanwhile, women's non-government organisations (NGOs) continue to be a much-needed legislative lobby, vocally monitoring government-friendliness to women. As Hillary Rodham Clinton pays tribute:

> *Time and again we have seen that it's NGOs who are responsible for making progress in any society . . . who have charted the real advances for women and children. It is the NGOs who have pressured governments . . . down the path to economic, social and political progress, often in the face of overwhelming hostility* (1996, p. 246).

Younger women are not only involved in these organisations – they lead them. At the helm of the YWCA of Australia – Australia's oldest existing women's organisation – are several strategic young women. Joint Presidents Susan Brennan and Lynda Poke are twenty-eight and thirty-two, while Acting Executive Officer Michelle Beg is twenty-four. Hardly yesterday's women. As leaders, they bring great skill to the organisation, applying their professional talents to non-paid work. Susan is barrister with an awesome attention to detail. During her last term on the National Executive, she rewrote the policy manual of the organisation (and, in the process, bolstered its feminist platform). Lynda runs her own accountancy practice and was the National Treasurer for two years before her election as President. She now oversees an ethical investment trust for the Association. Michelle is a journalism graduate whose writing skills are matched by her visual flair for layout and design. Through her efforts, the publications of the organisation are slick, professional productions.

As sites of power evolve and shift, feminist practice has expanded its agenda. In the 1970s and 1980s, the Women's Movement focused its attention on the role of the state.

This reflected the strong influence of government in almost all aspects of women's lives. The gamut of issues from pay equity to childcare, discrimination to health care, fertility control to affirmative action were regulated by legislation. These days we must be vigilant about the "old" rights in addition to providing a feminist presence in new spheres of influence, including the bastions of the private sector. Feminists are now required to be active on more fronts than ever before, in an era characterised by the extremes of work and a deepening sense of time poverty. These days we struggle to find time for relaxation, let alone activism. Thus, the professionalisation of feminism has been both a boon and a frustration. The grassroots activists of the 1970s became the femocrats of the 1980s and the consultants or managers of the 1990s – highly skilled women with strong networks and finances, but little time for lobbying.

If, as some commentators have suggested, some young women reject the collective, many others recognise its strategic vantage. Many find a stronger guarantee of gender equality in structural change than in the precedents of a solitary trailblazer. We know that our freedoms depend on legal rights which were won by well-coordinated lobbying campaigns. Rights can only be retained through their exercise and organised vigilance. And as this year's abortion debate in Western Australia demonstrated, those legal rights can be threatened at any time. So we still need a commitment to organised politics if we are to secure our gains.

Concurrently, younger women have great cause to be sceptical about the longevity and stability of celebrity clout. For a new breed of media-savvy, young feminists the risk is well-documented. We have watched the media create "golden girls" like Susan Ryan, Ros Kelly, Carmen Lawrence,

Bronwyn Bishop and Cheryl Kernot. They have been feted and hyped before the gloss starts to wear off and their credibility is attacked. Their individual tenure is no guarantee of women's basic rights.

Today, our brave new world requires us to translate important feminist concepts into soundbites, rather than lectures. These days the way to reach decision-makers is to influence markets. Accordingly, we need the skills to reach mass audiences with short messages, cultivating public sympathy or endorsement for our causes. That's why I rang the producers of *A Current Affair* in December, 1997 and challenged the Victorian President of the RSL, Bruce Ruxton to a televised debate about the republic and the flag.[2] A successful electoral strategy for our youth ticket was dependent upon broad commercial audiences, as well as our conventional alliances, if we were to make a difference.

This logic has also encouraged me over the past five years, to play "feminist" to my friend and talk-show host, Neil Mitchell at 3AW, the highest-rating morning show in metropolitan Melbourne. With a great deal of humour, we have discussed sexual harassment, sexist advertising on billboards, identifying discrimination and the need for women's organisations. Neil enjoys presenting the feminist position as unreasonable, prudish or petty to see what reaction he can provoke. I've found sustained humour and some jokes about insecure men of a certain age, with a paunch and facial hair to be effectively disarming.

---

2 Bruce Ruxton has been an outspoken opponent of changes to the Australian flag and the idea of a Republic. RSL is the acronym for the Returned Servicemen's League.

My political training came from three invaluable years in the student union movement, which taught me everything from writing a press release to running an election campaign, from negotiating to debating, from accosting strangers to understanding organisational processes. Those experiences didn't just give me a skillset for my professional life, they also provided a strong, close network of female friends. Many of the women who worked together on campus have continued to seek each other out, to work together on projects in the broader Women's Movement. Our friendships are fuelled by a similar interest in politics, although our party sympathies and memberships vary. We learn from each other constantly; giving feedback on public speeches, editing each other's published work and helping one another to strategise in our professional or political situations. And still very few social commentators recognise this new breed of feminists.

Throughout this decade many observers have declared feminism's death, gleefully reporting young women's hesitation to describe themselves as feminists. But their proclamations are wilfully ignorant. A generation schooled in symbolism knows both the power and constraints of labels. We'll use them when it's smart, but downplay them in more hostile forums. We are aware of the power of language to advocate, but also to stereotype, to limit and dismiss. We understand the power of the *f* word to connect us with our history and take pleasure in its loaded meanings and the hoary old stereotypes. When we first take on the mantle we tend to be earnest to a fault. Which of us can't recall ourselves ensconced in an impossible argument, using the particularly adamant tone of one who knows she is right? Later we learn to temper the gravity and to laugh at our detractors.

Social change demands organisation. No great feat has ever been achieved without strategy and coordination. Whether we are talking electoral politics or popular culture, the lessons are translatable: influence comes with a strategy for its acquisition, no matter how effortless power appears. At the end of the day, a girl's gotta have a plan. We can't afford to be naive if we are going to take our rightful share of power. We need to learn the skills of public influence if we hope to retain and exercise our rights. And we need to move from the politics of influence to the politics of governance. We must make the move from training lobbyists to grooming feminists for electoral power. In essence, we need to be coordinated, streetsmart and hard-nosed in our politics.

Meanwhile in the girlpower diary . . .
February, 1998
Old Parliament House, Canberra

> *After nine months of obsession, we took our places in history. I was one of the 152 delegates to the nation-shaping forum of the century, with a brief to speak for young Australians. The odds had been slim but we'd known enough about proportional representation to secure preferences across the field of candidates. I was still pinching myself to check it was real.*
>
> *And what a reality it was – the elder statespeople of Australian politics alongside novices, athletes and authors, war veterans and television producers, cattle farmers and clergy. All here to discuss the future shape of the nation.*
>
> *Two weeks of passionate dream-selling, story-telling and raw emotion. The indigenous intersecting the colonial, the aspirational meeting the nostalgic.*
>
> *And through the clamour rang the clear, articulate voices of young Australia, diverse in vision, but homogenous in passion. The young women, outnumbering the young men by two to one, gave us a taste of female power beyond the individual icon. Strong, sassy and streetsmart. Girlpower in action. Get used to it.*

Bibliography

American Psychiatric Association. (1994). *Diagnostic Statistical Manual of Mental Disorders.* Washington, D.C.: American Psychiatric Association.

Atwood, Margaret. (1972). *Lady Oracle.* London: Virago Press.

Bail, Kathy. (Ed.) (1996). *DIY Feminism.* Sydney: Allen and Unwin.

Benson, Elaine and John Esyen. (1996). *Unmentionables: A Brief History of Underwear.* New York: Simon and Schuster.

Berg, Elisa. (1996). Sisters and Solidarity: What's In A Grope? In Kathy Bail (Ed.) (1996). *DIY Feminism.* Sydney: Allen and Unwin.

Bernoth, A. (1997, May 14). Courts "Too Soft" on Home Violence, *Sydney Morning Herald,* 7.

Brown, Rita Mae. (1973). *Rubyfruit Jungle.* Plainfield, Vermont: Daughters.

Brownmiller, Susan. (1976). *Against Our Will, Men, Women and Rape.* London: Penguin Books.

Butler, Judith. (1990). *Gender Trouble: Feminism and the Subversion of Identity.* New York: Routledge.

Carter, Angela. (1983). Notes from the Frontline. In M. Wanda. (Ed.) (1983). *On Gender and Writing.* London: Pandora Press.

Chernin, Kim. (1981). *The Hungry Self: Women, Eating and Identity.* New York: Harper and Row.

Claflin, Tennessee. (1897). Virtue: What it is and What it is Not. *Talks and Essays.* Westminster: England. In Miriam Schneir (Ed.) (1992). *Feminism: The Essential Historical Writings.* New York: Vintage Books.

Clinton, Hillary Rodham. (1996). Opening Address. In Eva Friedlander (Ed.) (1996) *Look At the World Through Women's Eyes: Plenary Speeches from the NGO Forum on Women, Beijing 1995.* New York: Women Ink.

Curthoy, Ann. (1997). Where is Feminism Now. In Jenna Mead. (Ed.) (1997) *bodyjamming.* Sydney: Vintage.

de Beauvoir, Simone. (1959). *Memoirs of a Dutiful Daughter.* London: Penguin.

de Beauvoir, Simone. (1971). *The Second Sex.* (Translated and edited by H. M. Parshley.) London: Penguin Books; (1983) London: Picador.

de Lauretis, Teresa. (1987). *Technologies of Gender: Essays on Theory, Film and Fiction.* Bloomington: Indiana University Press.

de Pizan, Christine. (1405). *Le Livre de la Cité des Dammes.* (1982). *The Book of the City of Ladies.* (Translated by Earl Jeffrey Richards, foreword Marina Warner.) New York: Persea Books.

de Pizan, Christine. Eric Hicks. (Ed.) (1977). *Le Débat sur le Roman de la Rose.* Paris: Honoré Champion; (1978). (Translated and Edited by Joseph L. Baird and John R. Kane). *La Querelle de la Rose, Letters and Documents.* Chapel Hill: University of North Carolina Press.

Bibliography

Deluze, Gilles and Claire Parnet. (1987). *Dialogues*. New York: Columbia University Press.

Denfeld, Rene. (1995). *The New Victorians: A Young Woman's Challenge to the Old Feminist Order*. Sydney: Allen and Unwin.

Everisti, M. (1989). I am a feminist and . . . In Susan Sellers (Ed.) (1989) *Delighting the Heart*. London: The Women's Press.

Foucault, Michel. (1980). *The History of Sexuality Volume I: An Introduction*. New York: Pantheon.

Foucault, Michel. (1984). *The Use of Pleasure: The History of Sexuality Volume II*. New York: Penguin Books.

French, Marilyn. (1977). *The Women's Room*. New York: Ballantine Books.

Friedlander, Eva. (Ed.) (1996). *Look At the World Through Women's Eyes: Plenary Speeches from the NGO Forum on Women, Beijing 1995*. New York: Women Ink.

Friedberg, A. (1990). A Denial of Difference: Theories of Cinematic Identification. In E. A. Kaplan (Ed.) (1990) *Psychoanalysis and Cinema*. New York: Routledge.

Frye, Marilyn. (1992). *Willful Virgin*. California: The Crossing Press.

Frye, Marilyn. (1992). Willful Virgin *or* Do You Have to be a Lesbian to Be a Feminist? In Marilyn Frye (1992) *Willful Virgin*. California: The Crossing Press.

Garner, Helen. (1995). *The First Stone: Some Questions about Sex and Power*. Sydney: Picador.

Gatens, Moira. (1996). *Imaginary Bodies: Ethics, Power and Corporeality*. London: Routledge.

Gatens, Moira. (1996). Power, Bodies and Differences. In Moira Gatens (1996) *Imaginary Bodies: Ethics, Power and Corporeality*. London: Routledge.

George, Sheryn. (1996). The WARP Manifesto: Women are Real People. In Kathy Bail (Ed.) (1996) *DIY Feminism*. Sydney: Allen and Unwin.

George, Susan. (1988). *A Fate Worse than Debt*. London: Penguin.

Gillespie, Pat. (1998, January 17–18). Girl, Whore, Goddess, Dominatrix . . . *Weekend Aurstralian, Review*, 11.

Goldman, Emma. (1911/1972). Marriage and Love. In Alix Kates Shulman (Ed.) (1972) *Red Emma Speaks: Selected Writings and Speeches by Emma Goldman*. New York: Random House.

Greer, Germaine. (1997, October 16). The New Assault on Women, *Age*, A17.

Greer. Germaine. (1970). *The Female Eunuch*. London: Mac Gibbon and Key.

Griffin, Christine. (1993). *Representations of Youth*. Cambridge: Polity Press.

Grosz, E. (1990). Inscriptions and Body Maps: Representations and the Corporeal. In T. Threadgold and A. Cranny-Francis (Eds.) (1990) *Feminine/Masculine and Representation*. Sydney: Allen and Unwin.

Gunew, Sneja. (Ed.) (1990). *A Reader In Feminist Knowledge*. London: Routledge.

Harris, Laura and Elizabeth Crocker. (Eds.) (1997). *Fem(me): Feminist Lesbians Bad Girls*. New York: Routledge.

Harris, Laura and Elizabeth Crocker. (1997a). Bad Girls: Sex, Class and Feminist Agency. In Laura Harris and Elizabeth Crocker (Eds.) (1997) *Fem(me): Feminist Lesbians Bad Girls*. New York: Routledge.

Harris, Laura and Elizabeth Crocker. (1997b). An Introduction to Sustaining Femme Gender. In Laura Harris and Elizabeth Crocker (Eds.) (1997) *Fem(me): Feminist Lesbians Bad Girls*. New York: Routledge.

Hart, Nett. (1996). From an Eroticism of Difference to an Intimacy of Equals: A Radical Lesbian Separatist Perspective on Sexuality. In Lilian Mohin (Ed.) (1996) *An Intimacy of Equals*. London: Onlywomen Press.

Kaplan, E. A. (Ed.) (1990). *Psychoanalysis and Cinema*. New York: Routledge.

Kennedy, Elizabeth Lapovsky and Madeline Davis. (1994). *Boots of Leather, Slippers of Gold: The History of Lesbian Community*. New York: Penguin Books.

Kennedy, Elizabeth Lapovsky. (1997). The Hidden Voice: Femmes in the 1940s and 1950s. In Laura Harris and Elizabeth Crocker (Eds.) (1997) *Fem(me): Feminist Lesbians Bad Girls*. New York: Routledge.

Kong, Foo Ling. (1997). Outlaws in a Jam. In Jenna Mead (Ed.) (1997) *bodyjamming*. Sydney: Vintage.

Le Doeuff, Michele. (1991). *Hipparchia's Choice: An Essay Concerning Women, Philosophy, Etc.* Oxford: Basil Blackwell.

Lee, Bessie Harrison. (1903). Marriage and Heredity. In H. J. Osborn (1903) *Marriage, Heritage and the Social Evil*. London: National Temperance Publication Department.

Lumby, Catharine. (1997). *bad girls: the media, sex and feminism in the 90s*. Sydney: Allen and Unwin.

Maney, Mable. (1997). Mysteries, Mothers and Cops: An Interview with Mable Maney. In Laura Harris and Elizabeth Crocker (Eds.) (1997) *Fem(me): Feminist Lesbians Bad Girls*. New York: Routledge.

May, Jackie. (1996). The Beijing Conference and the Media, *The Australian Feminist Law Journal, 6*, 47–49.

McCowan, Lyndall. (1992). Re-collecting History, Renaming Lives: Femme Stigma and the Feminist Seventies and Eighties. In Joan Nestle (Ed) (1992) *The Persistent Desire: A Femme Butch Reader*. Boston, Massachusetts: Alyson Publications.

McLean, Paula. (1979). *Good Food for Babies and Toddlers*. Sydney: Angus and Robertson.

Mead, Jenna. (Ed.) (1997). *bodyjamming*. Sydney: Vintage.

Medhurst, Andy. (1997). Camp. In Andy Medhurst and Sally R. Munt. (Eds.) (1997) *Lesbian and Gay Studies: A Critical Introduction*. London: Cassell.

Medhurst, Andy and Sally R. Munt. (Eds.) (1997). *Lesbian and Gay Studies: A Critical Introduction.* London: Cassell.

Meyer, Moe. (1994). *The Politics and Poetic of Camp.* New York: Routledge.

Mohanty, Chandra Talpade. (1984). Under Western Eyes: Feminist Scholarship and Colonial Discourse, *boundary: A journal of Postmodern Literature and Culture, 2,* 333–39.

Mohin, Lilian. (Ed.) (1996). *An Intimacy of Equals: Lesbian Feminist Ethics.* London: Onlywomen Press.

Morris, Meaghan. (1997). Bodyjamming: Feminism and Public Life, *The Sydney Papers.* Sydney: The Sydney Institute.

Neill, Rosemary. (1995, June 24-25). The War Between the Women, *Weekend Australian,* 1–2.

Nestle, Joan. (Ed.) (1992). *The Persistent Desire: A Femme Butch Reader.* Boston, Massachusetts: Alyson Publications.

Newton, Esther. (1972). *Mother Camp: Female Impersonators in America.* Chicago: University of Chicago Press.

Nuttall, Merlyn and Sharon Morrison. (1997). *It Could Have Been You.* London: Virago Press.

Office of the Status of Women. (1993). A Woman's Perspective. In *Women in the Media: The National Working Party on the Portrayal of Women in the Media.* Canberra: AGPS.

Orford, Anne. (1997). Locating the International: Military and Monetary Interventions after the Cold War, *Harvard International Law Journal, 38,* (2).

Osborn, H. J. (1903). *Marriage, Heritage and the Social Evil.* London: National Temperance Publication Department.

Pratt, Minnie Bruce. (1997). Pronouns, Politics and Femme Practice: An Interview with Minnie Bruce Pratt. In Laura Harris and Elizabeth Crocker (Eds.) (1997) *Fem(me): Feminist Lesbians Bad Girls.* New York: Routledge.

Pybus, Cassandra. (1995, May 10). Examining a Photo is not Enough, *Sydney Morning Herald,* 16.

Reynolds, Margaret. (1993). *The Penguin Book of Lesbian Short Stories.* London: Penguin Books.

Rowland, Robyn. (Ed.) (1984). *Women Who Do and Women Who Don't Join the Women's Movement.* Sydney: Allen and Unwin.

Rugg, Rebecca Ann. (1997). How Does She Look? In Laura Harris and Elizabeth Crocker (Eds.) (1997) *Fem(me): Feminist Lesbians Bad Girls.* New York: Routledge.

Schneir, Miriam. (Ed.) (1992). *Feminism: The Essential Historical Writings.* New York: Vintage Books.

Schubert, Misha. (1995). Speech to the NGO Forum, Huairou.

Shulman, Alix Kales. (Ed.) (1972). *Red Emma Speaks: Selected Writings and Speeches by Emma Goldman.* New York: Random House.

Sellers, Susan. (Ed.) (1994). *Delighting the Heart: A Notebook by Women Writers.* London: The Women's Press.

Senate Economics References Committee. (1996). *Outworkers in the Garment Industry.* Unpublished Report: Commonwealth of Australia.

Sheehan, P. (1997, April 26). Right on, Sister. The Profile: Pru Goward, Feminist. *Sydney Morning Herald, Spectrum,* 3.

Sheridan, S. (1991). From Margin to Mainstream: Situating Women's Studies. In Sneja Gunew. (Ed.) (1990) *A Reader In Feminist Knowledge.* London: Routledge.

Shiva, Vandana. (1997). *Biopiracy: The Plunder of Nature and Knowledge.* Boston: South End Press.

Shulman, Alix Kates. (Ed.) (1972). *Red Emma Speaks: Selected Writings and Speeches by Emma Goldman.* New York: Random House.

Spivak, Gayatri Chakravorty. (1988). *In Other Worlds: Essays In Cultural Politics.* New York: Routledge.

Stamp, Patricia. (1994). Pastoral Power: Foucault and the New Imperial Order, *Arena Journal,* 11, 12.

Stanton, Theodore and Harriet Stanton Blanch, (1922). (Eds.) *Elizabeth Cady Stanton as Revealed in Her Letters, Diary and Reminiscences, 2.* New York: no publisher listed.

Stoltenberg, John. (1990). *Refusing to be a Man.* New York: Fontana.

Sykes, Roberta. (1984). Bobbie Sykes. In Robyn Rowland (Ed.) *Women Who Do and Women Who Don't Join the Women's Movement.* Sydney: Allen and Unwin.

Threadgold, T. and A. Cranny-Francis. (Eds.) (1990). *Feminine/Masculine and Representation.* Sydney: Allen & Unwin.

Trioli, Virginia. (1996). *Generation f: Sex, Power, and the Young Feminist.* Melbourne: Minerva.

United Nations World Conference on Women. (1995, September). *Youth Declaration.* Beijing.

United Nations. (1989). *United Nations Convention on the Rights of the Child.* New York: United Nations.

Walker, Alice. (1982). *The Color Purple.* New York: Harcourt Brace.

Walter, Natasha. (1998). *The New Feminism.* London: Little Brown and Company.

Wanda. M. (Ed.) (1993). *On Gender and Writing.* London: Pandora Press.

Winterson, Jeanette. (1993). Quoted in Margaret Reynolds. *The Penguin Book of Lesbian Short Stories.* London: Penguin Books.

Wolf, Naomi. (1990). *The Beauty Myth.* London: Vintage.

Bibliography

Wolf, Naomi. (1993). *Fire with Fire*. London: Chatto and Windus.

Wolf, Naomi. (1997). *Promiscuities: A Secret History of Female Desire*. London: Chatto and Windus.

Wollstonecraft, Mary. (1792). *A Vindication of the Rights of Women*; (1988). New York: W.W. Norton.

Woodhull, Victoria. (1873/1992). The Elixir of Life, or Why Do We Die? In Miriam Schneir (Ed.) (1992) *Feminism: The Essential Historical Writings*. New York: Vintage Books.

Woolf, Virginia. (1929). *A Room of One's Own*. London: The Hogarth Press.

XX. (1997). Sticks and Stones. In Jenna Mead (Ed.) (1997) *bodyjamming*. Sydney: Vintage.

YWCA. (1995). *Young Women Say Report*. Melbourne: YWCA of Australia.

Notes on Contributors

Cassandra Austin was raised on a large irrigation farm outside a tiny dustbowl of a town in NSW. She attended Melbourne University and gained her Masters Degree in Criminology. She worked as policy officer for a Commonwealth/State Ministerial Advisory Committee on Homelessness and for the Council to Homeless Persons. While a research fellow at Deakin University she was involved in projects on unemployment, respite care, child death and community service evaluation. She is now working in the United States as researcher and co-writer on her own documentary series.

Emily Ballou was born in Milwaukee, USA. She studied film and writing at the University of Wisconsin. In 1995, she completed a Masters in Women's Studies at the University of Sydney. She is a published poet and was awarded the Judith Wright Prize for Poetry at the 1997 Melbourne Writers' Festival. She is currently working on two feature film scripts. Emily lives in Kiama, NSW.

Samantha Brazel, the eldest of six sisters, has always been intimately interested in women's issues. After completing her Honours Degree in Communications at University of Technology Sydney in 1993, Samantha worked as an editorial assistant for Sydney-based client magazines before taking up work as a copy-editor at *Who Weekly* magazine.

Airlie Bussell completed her Higher School Certificate in Sydney in 1997. She is now studying Arts at the University of Sydney.

Rosie Cooney has been interested by and actively involved in feminist issues for several years. She studied law and biology at the Australian National University, and along the way was involved in Fems Rea, the feminist law student's group, was Women's Officer in the student government and wrote for *Woroni*, the student newspaper. She is currently studying for her PhD at the University of Cambridge, UK, on a Commonwealth Scholarship.

In 1997 **Louise D'Arcens** completed her PhD on gender and authority in the writings of medieval women through the English Department of the University of Sydney. She has also taught feminist courses in literature and cultural studies at a number of universities in Australia and the UK, and published articles on women's embodiment and literary practice. Currently, she is teaching literature in the School of English at Australian Defence Force Academy in Canberra.

Jo Dyer graduated in Law and Politics from the University of Adelaide in 1993. She was saved from a life in the law when offered a job as Assistant Producer with the State Theatre Company of South Australia. In 1995 she moved to Sydney to work with Mick Dodson at the Human Rights and Equal Opportunity Commission. She returned to the arts in 1996 and was appointed General Manager of Bangarra Dance Theatre in 1997. Jo is a long term devotee of the Australian Labor Party, and is a member of the Social Policy and Community Development National Policy Committee. In her spare time, she seeks to pacify the supervisor of her Masters of Arts.

Rosamund Else-Mitchell currently works in educational publishing in Sydney. She lived in the UK for five years where she completed an Honours Degree in English Literature and language at the University of Oxford. As Women's Officer of her college, she was involved with student union and feminist politics. In 1997 she graduated from the University of Sydney with a Masters in Women's Studies. She has worked as a secondary English teacher, an arts administrator, a bookseller, an actor, a theatre producer, a waitress and as a script editor variously in Oxford, London, Edinburgh and Sydney. Rosamund was born in 1970.

Ingrid FitzGerald completed an Honours Degree in Women's Studies at the Australian National University in 1992. She was the Coordinator of CAPOW! – the Coalition of Australian Participating Organisations of Women for two years and was appointed to the Australian Council for Women in 1993. Ingrid was awarded Young Canberra Citizen of the Year in 1994. Currently, she is a Senior Policy Officer for the NSW Committee on Ageing. She lives in Sydney.

Naomi Flutter has recently graduated with a Master of Public Policy from Harvard University's John F. Kennedy School of Government. She was the 1996 recipient of the Sir Edward Dunlop Memorial Award, presented by the Queen's Trust for Young Australians. While at university, Naomi sold jeans and worked as a research assistant. She has since been employed as a tutor at La Trobe University's law school and more recently in an investment bank. She is co-author of *Law As Culture*, an introductory student textbook about multiculturalism and the law, and co-editor of a fundraising anthology of refugee writings titled *Tilting Cages*. She has recently returned from Nepal where she facilitated creative writing workshops for Bhutanese refugees. Naomi has Honours Degrees in Law and Economics, and was born in 1970.

Stephanie Gilbert is employed by Centacare, Newcastle as a foster care broker. She is completing an MA in Women's Studies through Deakin University.

Krysti Guest is a human rights and international trade law adviser at the Commonwealth Parliamentary Research Service. She has previously worked at the Senate Legal and Constitutional Committee as a human rights adviser, at the Commonwealth Office of the Status of Women and the Attorney-General's Department. Krysti graduated with an Arts/Law Honours Degree from the University of Melbourne and is completing a Masters in International Law at the Australian National University. She is currently a key organiser of Australians for Native Title and Reconciliation in Canberra.

Tara Gutman, twenty-eight, is an entertainment lawyer in Sydney. She previously worked in two of Sydney's major commercial law practices. She has lived in Japan and travelled extensively in Cambodia, Vietnam and Burma. Tara sits on the management committee of the Australian Branch of the International Law Association and is an active member of its Human Rights Committee. She has recently learned to fly a single engine aeroplane.

Anita Harris lectures in Women's Studies at Deakin University, Geelong, Australia. She has an Honours Degree in Politics and Social Theory and a PhD in Politics from the University of Melbourne, Australia. She is currently researching the experiences of young women of South-East Asian origin growing up in Australia.

Galina Laurie was born in New Delhi, India, in 1970. She completed an Honours Degree at the University of Sydney in 1994, and is in the throes of a PhD on contemporary American academic women's autobiography. She has been published in several Australian journals. The child of itinerant Australian parents, she has travelled extensively in Asia, Europe and North America. She has been actively involved in queer culture and politics in Sydney for several years and has an extensive collection of nail polish.

Kate Lundy has lived in Canberra since she was six years-old, and at twenty-eight was elected an Australian Labor Party Senator for the Australian Capital Territory, after an early career in the construction industry and the union movement. In 1997, after just eighteen months in Parliament, she was promoted to the Opposition front bench as Shadow Parliamentary Secretary for Sport and Tourism, as well as assistant to the Shadow Ministers for Arts, Youth Affairs and Information Technology. She is a keen Internet surfer, watercolour painter and rower. She has two daughters Alexandra, aged seven, and Annabelle, aged three.

Ingrid McKenzie holds degrees in Economics and Law. She has worked as a legislative drafter, as a member of the now superseded Refugee Status Review Committee and for the Human Rights Branch of the Commonwealth Attorney-General's Department. Ingrid lives in Canberra with her partner Gary and their six month-old daughter, Hannah.

Virginia McLean has joined the thousands studying Arts at the University of Sydney. While she is definite that German, French and Linguistics are her interests, thinking about career prospects is definitely not. She would like to live in Sweden, dance in London, dream in Paris and eat in Italy.

Suzette Mitchell is currently working as the Gender In Development Specialist for the United Nations in Vietnam. She was a Doctoral student at the Australian National University in Political Science and Women's Studies. She worked for Snowy Mountains Electricity Commision International, as the first Gender and Development Specialist to be employed by an Australian commercial firm working in overseas development. She has also been known to adopt the identity of Veronika X for the local Canberra airwaves.

Misha Schubert has worked as a marketing consultant, social commentator and a community radio producer, before joining the staff of the *Australian* newspaper in Melbourne. In 1997, she was profiled by *Ms Magazine* as one of the twenty-one international young feminists to watch, and in 1998 was awarded the inaugural "Edna" young feminist of the year award. She sits on the Boards of YWCA of Australia, the YWCA Melbourne, Victorian Women's Trust and the Women's Electoral Lobby. In 1997, she co-founded the young republican organisation Republic4u, and was elected to the Commonwealth government's Constitutional Convention, advocating the views of younger Australians. She is twenty-five years old.

Debra Shulkes was born in 1975. She has been studying English and law for a few years too many at the University of Melbourne. She enjoys writing, and has published non-fiction and poetry in various magazines and journals. In 1994, her monologue *Playing Dead* was performed as part of the Melbourne New Wave festival. Since then, she has performed several readings of original works, most recently as part of the 1997 Melbourne Fringe Festival.

Louisa Smith is eighteen years-old. She is currently living in Germany teaching English. She hopes to return to Australia with clear ideas about what to study at university. In the meantime art and poetry continue to be her passions.

Vivienne Wynter is a media officer with an Australian Democrats' senator. She has a Bachelor's Degree in Journalism and Government from the University of Queensland. She has worked as a copywriter for a production company with unions, government departments and the Labor party as clients. Radio work followed, beginning as a stringer for Radio National's *Arts National*, and *Coming Out* programs and later in commercial radio newsrooms in Cairns and Brisbane.